THE PRIVATE DIARY OF
DR. JOHN DEE

Copyright © 2008 BiblioBazaar
All rights reserved

Original copyright: 1842

THE PRIVATE DIARY OF DR. JOHN DEE

And the Catalogue of His Library of Manuscripts

Edited by
JAMES ORCHARD HALLIWELL

BIBLIOBAZAAR

THE PRIVATE DIARY OF
DR. JOHN DEE

CONTENTS

PREFACE. 9

DR. DEE'S DIARY. 11

CATALOGUS. 75

A CATALOGUE OF SUCH OF DR. DEE'S MSS. AS ARE
    COME TO MY HANDS. 111

OTHER MANUSCRIPTS. 115

PREFACE.

The present volume contains two curious documents concerning Dr. Dee, the eminent philosopher of Mortlake, now for the first time published from the original manuscripts. I. His Private Diary, written in a very small illegible hand on the margins of old Almanacs, discovered a few years ago by Mr. W. H. Black, in the library of the Ashmolean Museum at Oxford. II. A Catalogue of his Library of Manuscripts, made by himself before his house was plundered by the populace, and now preserved in the library of Trinity College, Cambridge.

The publication of this Diary will tend perhaps to set Dee's character in its true light, more than any thing that has yet been printed. We have, indeed, his "Compendious Rehearsall," which is in some respects more comprehensive, but this was written for an especial purpose, for the perusal of royal commissioners, and he has of course carefully avoided every allusion which could be construed in an unfavourable light. In the other, however, he tells us his dreams, talks of mysterious noises in his chamber, evil spirits, and alludes to various secrets of occult philosophy in the spirit of a true believer. Mr. D'Israeli has given a correct and able view of his character in his "Amenities of Literature," which is remarkably confirmed in almost every point by the narrative now published. "The imagination of Dee," observes that elegant writer, "often predominated over his science; while both were mingling in his intellectual habits, each seemed to him to confirm the other. Prone to the mystical lore of what was termed the occult sciences, which in reality are no sciences at all, since whatever remains occult ceases to be science, Dee lost his better genius." I shall refer the reader to this popular work instead of attempting an original paper on the subject, which would necessarily be greatly inferior to that drawn by the masterly hand of the author of the "Curiosities of Literature."

The Catalogue of Dee's Library of Manuscripts, although long since dispersed, is valuable for the notices which it preserves of several middle-age treatises not now extant. He is said to have expended on this collection the sum of three thousand pounds, a very large sum in those days for a person of limited income.

J. O. H.

35, Alfred Place,

March 15th 1842.

DR. DEE'S DIARY.

1554. Aug. 25th, Barthilmew Hikman born at Shugborowh in Warwikshyre toward evening. My conjecture, uppon his own reporte of circumstances. Oct. 25th, D. Daniel Vander Meulen Antwerpiæ, mane hora quarta.[a]

a. It is almost unnecessary to observe that this and the following are notes of nativities. They are not for the most part contemporary notices, but apparently inserted at various times by Dee when professionally consulted as an astrologer.

1555. April 22nd, Jane Fromonds borne at Cheyham at none. Aug. 1st, Ed. Kelly natus hora quarta a meridie[b] ut annotatum reliquit pater ejus. Oct. 12th, the Lord Willughby born hora septima mane, ante meridiem, Lat. 51° 30', at Wesell in Gelderland.

b. "Anno 1555, Aug. 1, hora quarta a meridie Wigorniæ natus Dominus Edouardus Kelæus," MS. Ashm. 1788, fol. 140, where there is a horoscope of this nativity in the handwriting of Dr. Dee. Ashmole, in his MS. 1790, fol. 58, says "Mr. Lilly told me that John Evans informed him that he was acquainted with Kelly's sister in Worcester, that she shewed him some of the gold her brother had transmuted, and that Kelly was first an apothecary in Worcester."

1557. July 30th, Mr. Arundell of Cornwayle natus circa [horam] quartam a meridie.

1558. Dec. 14th, Mary Nevelle, alias Mary Lewknor, borne inter 11 et meridiem mane, by Chichester.

1560. July 8th, Margaret Russell, Cowntess of Cumberland, hora 2 min. 9 Exoniæ mane.

1561. Aug. 14th, Mr. Heydon, of Baconsthorp in Norfolk, hora noctis 11½ natus in comitatu Surrey.

1563. March 23rd, Mr. William Fennar a meridie inter horam undecimam et duodecimam nocte. June 23nd, Jane Cooper, now Mystris Kelly, toward evening. Sept. 28th, Mr. John Ask ante meridiem, by York six myle on this syde; Elizabeth Mownson, circa horam 9 mane, soror magistri Thomæ Mownson et uxor magistri Brown.

1564. Mrs. Brigit Cooke borne about seven of the clok on Saynt David's Day, which is the first day of March, being Wensday; but I cannot yet lerne whether it was before none or after. But she thinketh herself to be but 27 yeres old, anno 1593, Martii primo, but it cannot be so. June 20th, Mr. Hudson, hora septima ante meridiem. Aug. 21st, Wenefride Goose, inter 9 et 10 a meridie by Kingstone.

1565. Sept. 12th, John Pontoys, inter 9 et 10 ante meridiem prope Stony-Stratford; puto potius hora 8 min. 43. Oct. 17th, Thomas Kelley[c] hora quarta a meridie at Wurceter. Dec. 21st, Mr. Thomas Mownson at 11 of the clok in the morning.

c. The brother of the celebrated astrologer before mentioned.

1568. July 14th, William Emery born at Danbery in Essex paulo post undecimam horam noctis. Sept. 24th, Margaret Anderson mane inter 7 et 8.

1571. Samuel Swallow borne at Thaxstede in Essex Feb. 15 ante meridiem, inter horam undecimam et duodecimam, forte hora media post undecimam.

1575. July 31st, Simeon Stuard natus ante diluculum per horam 11½ at Shinfelde; his grandfather by the mother was Dr. Huyck the Quene's physicien.

1577. Jan. 16th, the Erle of Lecester, Mr. Phillip Sydney, Mr. Dyer, &c., came to my howse.[d] Jan. 22nd, The Erle of Bedford cam to my howse. Feb. 19th, great wynde S.W., close, clowdy. March 11th, my fall uppon my right nuckul bone, hora 9 fere mane; wyth oyle of Hypericon in 24 howres eased above all hope: God be thanked for such his goodness of his creatures! March 24th, Alexander Simon the Ninivite came to me, and promised me his servise into Persia. May 1st, I received from M. William Harbert of St. Gillian his notes uppon my Monas.[e] May 2nd, I understode of one Vincent Murfyn his abhominable misusing me behinde my back; Mr. Thomas Besbich told me his father is one of the cokes of the Court. May 20th, I hyred the barber of Cheswik, Walter Hooper, to kepe my hedges and knots in as good order as he sed them than, and that to be done with twise cutting in the yere at the least and he to have yerely five shillings, [and] meat and drink. June 10th, circa 10, a shower of hayle and rayne. June 18th, borrowed £40 of John Hilton of Fulham. June 19th, I understode of more of Vincent Murfyn his knavery; borrowed £20 of Bartylmew Newsam. June 20th, borow £27 uppon the chayn of golde. June 26th, Elen Lyne gave me a quarter's warning. June 27th, showrs of rayne and hayle. Aug. 19th, the Hexameron Brytanicum[f] put to printing.

d. "Dr. Dee dwelt in a house neere the water side, a little westward from the church [at Mortlake. The buildings which Sir Fr. Crane erected for working of tapestry hangings, and are still (1673) employed to that use, were built upon the ground whereon Dr. Dee's laboratory and other roomes for that use stood. Upon the west is a square court, and the next is the house wherein Dr. Dee dwelt, now inhabited by one Mr. Selbury, and further west his garden."—MS. Ashm. 1788, fol. 149. The same account says that "Dr. Dee was wel beloved and respected of all persons of quality thereabouts, who very often invited him to their houses or came to his."

e. This of course is his celebrated Monas Hieroglyphica, frequently printed, and the nature of which I attempted to explain in a paper read before the Society of Antiquaries. Mr. Herbert, according to MS. Ashm. 1788, "dwelt then in Mortlack and was an intimate friend of Dr. Dee's."

f. This was his work printed in 1577 under the title of General and Rare Memorials pertayning to the perfect Art of Navigation, in folio, now a book of the greatest rarity. The original manuscript of it is in MS. Ashm. 1789, and Dee's own copy of the published work with MS. notes and additions is preserved in the British Museum. In his Letter Apological, 4to. Lond. 1603, he cites this work under the title of The Brytish Monarchie, as having been written in the year 1576.

Nov. 3rd, William Rogers of Mortlak, abowt 7 of the clok in the morning, cut his own throte, by the fende his instigation. Nov. 6th, Sir Umfrey Gilbert cam to me to Mortlak. Nov. 18th, borowed of Mr. Edward Hynde of Mortlak £30 to be repayed at Hallowtyde next yere. Nov. 20th, two tydes in the forenone, the first 2 or 3 howres to sone. Nov. 22nd, I rod to Windsor to the Q. Majestie. Nov. 25th, I spake with the Quene hora quinta. Nov. 28th, I spake with the Quene hora quinta; I spake with Mr. Secretary Walsingham.[g] I declared to the Quene her title to Greenland, Estetiland and Friseland.

g. Ashmole informs us that Walsingham continued for a length of time one of Dr. Dee's best patrons.

Dec. 1st, I spake with Sir Christofer Hatton; he was made knight that day. Dec. 1st, I went from the cowrte at Wyndsore. Dec. 30th, inexplissima illa calumnia de R. Edwardo, iniquissime aliqua ex parte in me denunciabatur: ante aliquos elapsos dies, sed . . . sua sapientia me innocentem.

1578. Feb. 5th, sponsalia cum Jana Fromonds horam circiter primam. April 28th, I caused Sir Rowland Haywood to examyn Francys Baily of his sklandering me, which he denyed utterly. June 13th, rayn and in the afternone a little thunder. June 30th, I told Mr. Daniel Rogers,[h] Mr. Hackluyt of the Middle Temple being by, that Kyng Arthur and King

Maty, both of them, did conquier Gelindia, lately called Friseland, which he so noted presently in his written copy of Monumethensis,[i] for he had no printed boke therof. July 14th, my sister Elizabeth Fromonds cam to me. July 27th, hora 9, min. 15 a meridie Francis Cowntess of Hertford.

h.   Rogers was a member of the University of Oxford, and a large commonplace-book in his handwriting is in Archbishop Tenison's library in St. Martin's-in-the-Fields.

i.   That is, Galfridus Monumetensis de gestis regum Britanniæ. Hackluyt mentions this fact in his collection of voyages.

Aug. 5th, Mr. Raynolds of Bridewell tok his leave of me as he passed toward Darthmowth to go with Sir Umfry Gilbert toward Hocheleya. Aug. 15, I went toward Norwich with my work of Imperium Brytanicum. [k] Aug. 23rd, I cam to London from Norwich. Aug. 31st, I went to my father-in-law Mr. Fromonds to Cheyham.

k.   This is the book just mentioned under the title of General and Rare Memorials, fol. Lond. 1577.

Sept. 1st, I cam from Cheyham. Sept. 6th, Elen Lyne, my mayden, departed from this life immediately after the myd-day past, when she had lyne sik a month lacking one day. Sept. 12th, Jane Gaele cam to my servyce, and she must have four nobles by the yere, 26s. 8d. Sept. 25th, Her Majestie cam to Richemond from Grenwich. Sept. 26, the first rayn that came for many a day; all pasture abowt us was withered: rayn afternone like Aprill showres. Oct. 8th, the Quene's Majestie had conference with me at Richemond inter 9 et 11. Oct. 16th, Dr. Bayly conferred of the Quene her disease. Oct. 22nd, Jane Fromonds went to the court at Richemond. Oct. 25th, a fit from 9 afternone to 1 after mydnight. Oct. 28, the Erle of Lecester and Sir Francys Walsingham, secretary, determined my going over for the Quene's Majestie. Nov. 4th,

I was directed to my voyage by the Erle of Lecester and Mr. Secretary Walsingham hora nona. Nov. 7th, I cam to Gravesende. Nov. 9th, I went from Lee to sea. Nov. 14th, I cam to Hamburgh hora tertia. Dec. 11th, to Franckfurt-uppon-Oder. Dec. 15th, newes of Turnifer's comming hora octava mane, by a speciall mesenger.

1579. A moyst Marche and not wyndy. June 10th, I shewed to Mr. John Lewis and his sonne, the physition, the manner of drawing aromaticall oyles. At that tyme my cat got a fledge yong sparrow which had onely a right wyng naturally. June 15th, my mother surrendred Mortlak howses and land, and had state geven in plena curia ad terminum vitæ, and to me was also the reversion delivered per virgam, and to my wife Jane by me, and after to my heirs and assignes for ever, to understand, Mr. Bullok and Mr. Taylor, surveyor, at Wimbledon, under the tree by the church. June 22nd, Mr. Richard Hickman and Barthilmew his nephew cam to me with Mr. Flowr, commended by Mr. Vicechamberlayn Sir Christopher Hatton.

July 6th, Mr. Hitchcok, who had travayled in the plat for fishing, made acquayntance with me, and offred me great curtesy.

July 13th, Arthurus Dee natus[1] puer mane hor. 4 min. 30 fere, vel potius min. 25, in ipso ortu solis, ut existimo. After 10 of the clock this night my wive's father Mr. Fromonds was speechles, and died on Tuesday (July 14th) at 4 of the clock in the morning. July 16th, Arthur was christened at 3 of the clok afternone; Mr. Dyer and Mr. Doctor Lewys, judg of the Admiralty, were his godfathers; and Mistres Blanche Pary of the Privie Chamber his godmother. But Mr. John Harbert of Estshene was deputy for Dr. Lewys, and Mystres Awbrey was deputy for my cosen Mistres Blanche Pary.

1. His horoscope is in MS. Ashm. 1788. "Mr. Arthur Dee's birth was accompanied by the unhappy accident of the death of Mr. Fromonds, his mother's father, who died that morning."—MS. Ashm. 1790, fol. 63.

Aug. 8th, John Elmeston,ᵐ student of Oxford, cam to me for dialling. Aug. 9th, Jane Dee churched. Aug. 16th, Monsieur cam secretly to the court from Calays. Aug. 20th, wyndy, clowdy, rayny. Aug. 26, Monsieur went back agayn to France. Sept. 10th, my dream of being naked, and my skyn all overwrowght with work like some kinde of tuft mockado, with crosses blew and red; and on my left arme, abowt the arme, in a wreath, this word I red—sine me nihil potestis facere: and another the same night of Mr. Secretary Walsingham, Mr. Candish, and myself.

m. This person is not noticed by the Oxford biographers.

Oct. 3rd, Sir Leonel Ducket his unkend letter for mony. Oct. 4th, goodman Hilton requested me for his ij. sonnes to resort to my howse. Oct. 5th, raging wynde at West and Southerly, in the night chefely. Oct. 9th, 10th, 11th, 12th, great rayne for three or four dayes and nights. Oct. 13th, this day it broke up; the fote bote for the ferry at Kew was drowned and six persons, by the negligens of the ferryman overwhelming the boat uppon the roap set there to help, by reason of the vehement and high waters. Oct. 18th, Mr. Adrian Gilbert and John Davys reconcyled themselves to me, and disclosed some of Emery his most unhonest, hypocriticall, and devilish dealings and devises agaynst me and other, and likewise of that errant strompet her abominable wordes and dedes; and John Davis sayd that he might curse the tyme that ever he knew Emery, and so much followed his wicked cownsayle and advyse. So just is God! Oct. 31st, payed xxs fyne for me and Jane my wife to the Lord of Wimbleton (the Quene), by goodman Burton of Putney, for the surrender taken of my mother of all she hath in Mortlak to Jane and me, and than to my heyres and assynes, &c.

Nov. 25th, the Lord Clinton cam to me and offred Skirbeck by Boston for Long Lednam. Nov. 29th, I receyved a letter from Mr. Thomas Jones. Dec. 9th, Θις νιγτ μι υυιφ δρεμιδ θατ ονε καμ το ἑρ ανδ τουχεδ ἑρ, σαιινγ, "Μιστρες Δεε, γου αρ κονκειυεδ οφ χιλδ, ὑος ναμε μυστ βε Ζαχαριας; βε οφ γυδ χερε, ἐ σαλ δο υυελ ας θις δοθ!"ⁿ Dec. 22nd, I payd Jane 13*s*. and 4*d*. for her wagys tyll Michelmas last, for the half yere, so that I owe her yet *6s. 8d*. Dec. 28th, I reveled to Roger Coke° the gret secret of the elixir of the salt οφ ακετελς ονε υππον α υνδρεδ

n. Dee has occasionally made use of Greek letters for the preservation of his notes, still retaining the English language. The present passage may as well be given:—"This night my wife dreamed that one cam to her and touched her, saying, 'Mistres Dee, you are conceived of child, whose name must be Zacharias; be of good chere, he sal do well as this doth!'"
o. In a more appropriate place I shall give from an Ashmolean manuscript a traditionary anecdote relating to this Roger Coke, or Cooke, and the great secret which Dee revealed to him.

1580. Jan. 13th, I gave my wife mony for the month. Jan. 16th, Arthur fell sick, stuffed with cold fleym, could not slepe, had no stomach to eat or drink as he had done before. Feb. 26th, this night the fyre all in flame cam into my maydens chamber agayne, betwene an eleven and twelve of the cloke; contynued half an howr terribly, so it did a yere before to the same maydens, Mary Cunstable and Jane Gele. May 17th, at the Moscovy howse for the Cathay voyage. June 3rd, Mr. A. Gilbert and J. Davys rod homward into Devonshire. June 7th, Mr. Skydmor and his wife lay at my howse and Mr. Skydmor's dowghter, and the Quene's dwarf Mrs. Tomasin. June 8th, my wife went with Mistres Skydmor to the court. June 12th, Mr. Zackinson and Mr. Cater lay at my howse, having supped at my Lady Crofts. June 14th, Mr. Fosku of the Wardrip lay at my howse, and went the next day to London with Mr. Coweller. July 15th, the Lady Croft went from Mortlak to the court at Otlands. June 30th, payd Jane *20s*. for thre quarters' wages, so that all that is due is payd, and all other recknengs likewise is payd her *6s. 8d*.; and Mary Constable was payd all old reknings 15*s*., and my wife had eleven pounds to dischardge all for thirteen wekes next, that is, till the 5th of November: I delivered Mr.

Williams, the person of Tendring, a lettre of atturney agaynst one White of Colchester, for a sklaundre.

Aug. 27th, Arthur was weaned this night first. Aug. 28th, my dealing with Sir Humfrey Gilbert for his graunt of discovery. Aug. 30th, Nurse Darant was discharged and had 10s. given her, which was the whole quarter's wages due at a fortnight after Michelmas.

Sept. 6th, the Quene's Majestie cam to Richemond. Sept. 10th, Sir Humfry Gilbert graunted me my request to him, made by letter, for the royaltyes of discovery all to the North above the parallell of the 50 degree of latitude, in the presence of Stoner, Sir John Gilbert, his servant or reteiner; and thereuppon toke me by the hand with faithfull promises in his lodging of John Cooke's howse in Wichcross strete, where wee dyned onely us three together, being Satterday. Sept. 13th, Mr. Lock browght Benjamyn his sonne to me: his eldest sonne also, called Zacharie, cam then with him. Sept. 17th, the Quene's Majestie cam from Rychemond in her coach, the higher way of Mortlak felde, and whan she cam right against the church she turned down toward my howse: and when she was against my garden in the felde she stode there a good while, and than cam ynto the street at the great gate of the felde, where she espyed me at my doore making obeysains to her Majestie; she beckend her hand for me; I cam to her coach side, she very speedily pulled off her glove and gave me her hand to kiss; and to be short, asked me to resort to her court, and to give her to wete when I cam ther; hor. 6¼ a meridie. Sept. 14th, I began against Vincent Murphyn. Sept. 15th, I wrote to the bishop of London. Sept. 22nd, my declaration against Vincent Murphin put into the court of Geldhall.

Oct. 3rd, on Munday, at 11 of the clok before none, I delivered my two rolls of the Quene's Majesties title unto herself in the garden at Richemond, who appointed after dynner to heare furder of the matter. Therfore betwene one and two afternone, I was sent for into her highnes Pryvy Chamber, where the Lord Threasurer also was, who, having the matter slightly then in consultation, did seme to dowt much that I had or could make the argument probable for her highnes' title so as I pretended. Wheruppon I was to declare to his honor more playnely, and at his leyser, what I had sayd and could say therin, which I did on Tuesday and Wensday following, at his chamber, where he used me very honorably on his behalf. Oct. 7th, on Fryday I cam to my Lord Threasorer, and he being told of my being without, and allso I standing before him at his comming furth, did not or would not speak to me, I dowt not of some new greif conceyved. Oct. 10th, the Quene's Majestie, to my great cumfort (hora quinta), cam with her trayn from the court and at my dore graciously calling me to her, on horsbak, exhorted me briefly to take my mother's death patiently, and withall told me that the Lord Threasorer had gretly commended my doings for her title, which he had to examyn, which title in two rolls he had browght home two howrs before; she remembred allso how at my wive's death it was her fortune likewise to call upon me.ᴾ At 4 of the clok in the morning my mother Jane Dee dyed at Mortlak; she made a godly ende: God be praysed therfore! She was 77 yere old. Oct. 20th, I had by my jury at Geldhall £100 damages awarded me against Vincent Murphyn the cosener. Oct. 22nd, with much ado I had judgment against Murfin at Geldhall. My mervaylous horsnes and in manner spechelesnes toke me, being nothing at all otherwise sick. Oct. 25th, Morrice Kyffin departed from me with my leave. Nov. 2nd, the Lord Threasorer sent me a haunche of venison. Thomas Suttley had the bishop of Canterbury his letter for Sir Richard. Nov. 3rd, I writt to my Lord Threasurer. Nov. 6th, Helen cam to my servyse. Nov. 12th, somwhat better in my voyce. Nov. 22nd, the blasing starᵍ I cold see no more, though it were a cler night. Dec. 1st, newes cam by Dr. Deny from Ireland of the Italiens overthrow whom the Pope had sent, the Quene lying at Richemond. Dec. 6th, the Quene removed from Richmond. Dec. 8th, recepi literas Roma, scriptas per fratrem Laudervicea.

p.   His first wife died on the 16th of March 1575, when "the Queen's Majestie, with her most honourable Privy Council, and other her Lords and Nobility, came purposely to have visited my library. but finding that my wife was within four houres before buried out of the house, her Majestie refused to come in; but willed to fetch my glass so famous, and to show unto her some of the properties of it, which I did; her Majestie being taken down from her horse by the Earle of Leicester, Master of the Horse, at the church wall of Mortlake, did see some of the properties of that glass, to her Majestie's great contentment and delight."—*Compendious Memorial*, p. 516. This glass is spoken of again.

q. Dee has made a rough sketch of the appearance of this comet, with its long tail, on the margin of the MS.

1581.ʳ Feb. 9th, I agreed with Mr. Gentle Godolphin for to release the coosener Vincent Murphin. Feb. 11th, Harry Prise, of Lewsam, cam to me at Mortlak, and told of his dreames often repeated, and uppon my prayer to God this night, his dreame was confirmed, and better instruction given. Feb. 12th, Sir William Harbert cam to Mortlak. Feb. 23rd, I made acquayntance with Joannes Bodinus, in the Chambre of Presence at Westminster, the embassador being by from Monsieur. Feb. 26th, a very fayr calm warm day.

r. An original diary of the chemical experiments made by Dr. Dee in this year is preserved in the Bodleian Library.—MS. Rawl. Miscel. 241.

March 8th, it was the 8 day, being Wensday, hora noctis 10, 11, the strange noyse in my chamber of knocking; and the voyce, ten tymes repeted, somewhat like the shrich of an owle, but more longly drawn, and more softly, as it were in my chamber. March 12th, all reckenings payd to Mr. Hudson, £11. 17*s*. March 13th, Elizabeth Kyrton cam to my servys. March 23rd, at Mortlak cam to me Hugh Smyth, who had returned from Magellan straights and Vaygatz; after that, raynie, stormie wynde, S.W.

March 25th, Helen was hyred at our Lady day for the yere for fowr nobles wagis; she had her covenant peny, and allso vj*s* viij*d*. for her payns taken synce she came. April 3rd, I ryd toward Snedgreene, to John

Browne, to here and see the manner of the doings. April 14th, I cam home from Snedgreene. May 25th, I had sight in +Chrystallô+ offerd me, and I saw. June 7th, hora 7½ mane nata est Katharina Dee. June 10th, baptisata a meridie hor. 5½ Katharina. Mr. Packington of the court, my Lady Katarin Crofts, wife to Sir James Crofts, Mr. Controller of the Quene's household, Mystres Mary Skydmor of the Privie Chamber, and cosen to the Quene, by theyr deputies christened Katharin Dee. June 17th, yong Mr. Hawkins, who had byn with Sir Francis Drake, cam to me to Mortlake. June 30th, Mr. John Leonard Haller, of Hallerstein, by Worms in Germany, receyved his instructions manifold for his jornay to Quinsay, which jornay I moved him unto, and instructed him plentifully for the variation of the compas, observing in all places as he passed.

July 6th, my wife churched. July 7th, in the morning at 1¾ after mydnight, Mr. Hinde his sonne born. July 10th, my right sholder and elbow-joynt were so extremely in payn that I was not able in 14 dayes to lift my arme owtward not an ynche; the payn was extreme; I used Mr. Larder, Mr. Alles, and Alise Davyes, and abowt the 25 day I mended. July 12th, abowt 10 of the clock ½ before noone Ebtre uvf vaperqvoyr qbttrqarf naq vatengrshyarf ntnvaf zr gb zv fnpr nyzbfg erqv gb ynl ivbyrag unaqf ba zr, zntre uraevk pna cnegryv gry. At the same day the Erle of Lecester fell fowly owt with the Erle of Sussex, Lord Chamberlayn, calling each other traytor, whereuppon both were commanded to kepe theyr chambers at Greenwich, wher the court was. July 19th, Mr. Henrick went to London to visit his wife and children. July 26th, Mr. Haylok cam, and goodman King with him. July 28th, Mr. Collens did ride into Lincolneshire.

Aug. 3rd, all the night very strange knocking and rapping in my chamber. Aug. 4th, and this night likewise. Katharin was sent home from nurse Maspely, of Barnes, for fear of her mayd's sicknes, and goodwife Benet gave her suck. Aug. 11th, Katharine Dee was shifted to nurse Garret at Petersham on Fryday, the next day after St. Lawrence day, being the 11th day of the month; my wife went on foot with her, and Ellen

Cole, my mayd, George and Benjamin, in very great showres of rayn. Aug. 12th, recepi literas a D. Doctore Andrea Hess occultæ philosophiæ studioso, per Richardi Hesketh amici mei, Antwerpiæ agentis, diligentiam in negociis meis, et recepi, una cum literis, Mercurii Mensitam seu Sigillam Planetarum. Aug. 26th, abowt 8½ (at night) a strange meteore in forme of a white clowde crossing galaxiam, whan it lay north and sowth over our zenith; this clowd was at length from the S.E. to the S.W. sharp at both endes, and in the west ende it was forked for a while; it was abowt sixty degrees high, it lasteth an howr, all the skye clere abowt, and fayr starshyne.

Sept.[s] 5th, Roger Cook, who had byn with me from his 14 yeres of age till 28, of a melancholik nature, pycking and devising occasions of just cause to depart on the suddayn, abowt 4 of the klok in the afternone requested of me lycense to depart, wheruppon rose whott words between us; and he, imagining with hisself that he had the 12 of July deserved my great displeasure and finding himself barred from vew of my philosophicall dealing with Mr. Henrik, thowght that he was utterly recest from intended goodnes toward him. Notwithstanding Roger Cook his unseamely dealing, I promised him, yf he used himself toward me now in his absens, one hundred pounds[t] as sone as of my own clene hability I myght spare so much; and moreover, if he used himself well in lif toward God and the world, I promised him some pretty alchimicall experiments, whereuppon he might honestly live. Sept. 7th, Roger Cook went for alltogether from me. Sept. 29th, Robert Gardner, of Shrewsbury, cam to my servyce.

s. Dr. Dee, in the Rawlinson MS. just quoted, observes, in his notes on this month, "Mr. Harry Waters went away the 2nd day, malcontent. John Dee, Jesus bless me!"

t. This probably gave rise to the anecdote which is related in MS. Ashm. 1788, fol. 147, viz. that "he revealed to one Roger Cooke the great secret of the elixar, as he called it, of the salt of metalls, the projection whereof was one upon an hundred."

Oct. 8th, I had newes of the chests of bokes fownd by Owndle in Northamptonshyre; Mr. Barnabas Sawle told me of them, but I fownd no truth in it. Oct. 9th, Barnabas Saul, lying in the . . . hall was strangely trubled by a spirituall creature abowt mydnight. Oct. 13th, I rod to Sowth Myms. Oct. 14th, to St. Nedes. Oct. 16th, at Mr. Hikman's. Oct. 20th, at Tosseter. Oct. 21st, Oxford, Dr. Cradocke. Oct. 23rd, from Oxford to Wyckam. Oct. 24th, I cam home. Robert Hilton cam to my service. Nov. 16th, the Quene removed to White Hall, and Monsieur with her. Nov. 27th, I rod to Greensede. Nov. 28th, to goodman Wykham, 2 myles beyond Chayly by Lewys. Nov. 29th, I made acquayntance with Mr. George Kylmer for Sir George his bokes. Nov. 30th, I cam home. Dec. 1st, Katharyn Dee her nurse was payd 6s. so nothing is owing to her. Dec. 5th, Elen my mayden fell sick. Dec. 7th, George my man had the great fall of the ladder, hora 10 fere mane. Dec. 8th, I sent a letter to Mr. Kylmer. Dec. 22nd, my Lord Chanceler's sonne, Mr. Bromley, and Sir William Herbert cam to me. Helen Cole was payd her wages and reckening tyll this Christmas, and so discharged my servyce, being newly recovered of her ague. Her desyre was to go to her frendes.

1582. Jan. 11th, Robert Gardener desired my leave to go dwell with Sir William Herbert, hora 12. Jan. 16th, Mistris Harbert cam to Essexe. Jan. 17th, Randal Hatton cam home from Samuel's father at Stratton Audley. Jan. 22nd, Arthur Dee and Mary Herbert, they being but 3 yere old the eldest, did make as it wer a shew of childish marriage, of calling ech other husband and wife. Jan. 22, 23rd. The first day Mary Herbert cam to her father's hous at Mortlak, and the second day she cam to her father's howse at Estshene. Jan. 23rd, my wife went to nurse Garret and payd her for this month ending the 26 day. Jan. 27th, Barnabas Sawl his brother cam. Feb. 12th, abowt 9 of the clok, Barnabas Saul and his brother Edward went homward from Mortlak: Saul his inditement being by law fownd insufficient at Westminster Hall: Mr. Serjeant Walmesley, Mr. Owen and Mr. Hyde, his lawyers at the bar for the matter, and Mr. Ive, the clerk of the Crown Office, favouring the other. Feb. 20th, Mr. Bigs of Stentley by Huntingdon and John Littlechild cam to me. I receyved a letter from Barnabas Saul. Feb. 21st, Mr. Skullthorp rod toward Barnabas. Feb. 25th, Mr. Skulthorp cam home. Payd nurse Garret for Katharin tyll Fryday the 23 day, vj.s. then somethyng due to nurse for iij. pownd of candell and 4 pownd of sope.

March 1st, Mr. Clerkson browght Magnus to me at Mortlak, and so went that day agayn. March 6th, Barnabas Saul cam this day agayn abowt one of the clok and went to London the same afternone. He confessed that he neyther hard or saw any spirituall creature any more. March 8th, Mr. Clerkson and his frende cam to my howse. Barnabas went home agayn abowt 3 or 2 clok, he lay not at my howse now; he went, I say, on Thursday, with Mr. Clerkson. March 8th, coelum ardere et instar sanguinis in diversis partibus rubere visum est circa horam nonam noctis, maxime versus septentrionalem et occidentalem partem: sed ultra capita nostra versus austrum frequenter miles quasi sanguineus. March 9th, Fryday at dynner tyme Mr. Clerkson and Mr. Talbot[v] declared a great deale of Barnabas nowghty dealing toward me, as in telling Mr. Clerkson ill things of me that I should mak his frend, as that he was wery of me, that I wold so flatter his frende the lerned man that I wold borow him of him. But his frend told me, before my wife and Mr. Clerkson, that a spirituall creature told him that Barnabas had censured both Mr. Clerkson and me. The injuries which this Barnabas had done me diverse wayes were very great. March 22nd, Mr. Talbot went to London, to take his jornay.

v. Just above this relation some one has written, "you that rede this underwritten assure yourselfe that yt is a shamfull lye, for Talbot neither studied for any such thinge nor shewed himselfe dishonest in any thinge." Dr. Dee has thus commented upon it:—"This is Mr. Talbot or that lerned man, his own writing in my boke, very unduely as he cam by it." There are several other notices of

Talbot erased, but whether by him or by the Doctor it is impossible to say, but most probably the former.

April 16th, Nurse Garet had her *6s.* for her month ending on the 20th day. April 22nd, a goodly showr of rayn this morning early. May 4th, Mr. Talbot went. May 13th, Jane rod to Cheyham. May 15th, nocte circa nonam cometa apparuit in septentrione versus occidentem aliquantulum; cauda versus astrum tendente valde magna, et stella ipsa vix sex gradus super horizontem. May 20th, Robertus Gardinerus Salopiensis lætum mihi attulit nuncium de materia lapidis, divinitus sibi revelatus de qua . . . May 23rd, Robert Gardener declared unto me hora 4½ a certeyn great philosophicall secret, as he had termed it, of a spirituall creatuer, and was this day willed to come to me and declare it, which was solemnly done, and with common prayer. May 28th, Mr. Eton of London cam with his son-in-law Mr. Edward Bragden, as concerning Upton parsonage, to have me to resign or let it unto his said son-in-law, whom I promised to let understand whenever myself wold consent to forego it. June 9th, I writ to the Archbishop of Canterbury a letter in Latin: Mr. Doctor Awbrey did carry it. June 14th, Morryce Kyffin did viset me. June 22nd, Nurse Garret had *6s.* for a month ending the 18 day of May; she is to have for a month wages ending the 15 day of this June. My wife went this Friday thither with Benjamyn. June 27th, Mystris Stafford arrested me hora 11: I payd all.

July 3rd, hor. 12¼, Arthur Dee fell from the top of the Water-gate Stayres down to the fote from the top, and cut his forhed on the right eyebrow. Sir Richard browght the rent. July 6th, in feare of resting by proctor Lewys: tyll 9½ at night from 1 afternone at the Docter's comming. July 12th, Proctor Lewys agred withall. July 13th, Mr. Talbot cam abowt 3 of the clok afternone, with whom I had some wordes of unkendnes: we parted frendely: he sayd that the Lord Morley had the Lord Mountegle his bokes. He promised me some of Doctor Myniver's bokes. July 16th, Mr. William Pole, whome Phillip Simons, somtymes barber to the old Erle of Tavistok, doth knowe, cam to me, and made acquayntance with me: promised to com agayn within xiiij. dayes. Jane my wife went to Nurse Garret's to pay her 12*s*. for her wages due tyll Friday last, which was Saint Margaret's day, and brought her xijd. for candles: she went by water; Mistres Lee went with her, and Robyn Jackesbite. Jane this night was sore trubbled with a collick and cramp in her belly; she vomyted this Monday more, and every night grew stiff in the sole likewise. A meridie hor. 3½ cam Sir George Peckham to me to know the tytle for Norombega in respect of Spayn and Portugall parting the whole world's distilleryes. He promysed me of his gift and of his patient . . . of the new conquest, and thought to get so moche of Mr. Gerardes gift to be sent me with seale within a few days. July 18th, Barthilmew Knaresburgh his sone borne at break of day abowt 3 of the clok. June 19th, Barnabas Saul came to see me at Mortlak: I chyd hym for his manifold untrue reports. July 23d, Mistris Franklin's sone borne at noone. July 24th, Robert Gardiner cam, and went on the 26th.

Aug. 8th, Kate was sickly. Aug. 11th, Mr. Bacon and Mr. Phillips of the court cam. Aug. 20th, Katarine still seemed to be diseasid. Aug. 25th, Katharin was taken home from nurse Garret of Petersham, and weaned at home. Aug. 31st, Benjamin Lock told me of his father's mynde to send him to Spayn within three or four days. Sept. 1st, I did for Sir John Killegrew devise the way of protestation to save him harmless for compounding with Spaniard who was robbed: he promised me fish against Lent. Sept. 10th, Mr. John Leonard Haller, of Hallersteyn, by Worms in Germany, cam agayn to me, to declare his readines to go toward Quinsay; and how he wold go and ly at Venys all this winter, and from thens to Constantinople. I requested Mr. Charles Sted to help him to make his mony over to Paris and Nuremberg, and to help him with the sercher of Rye to pass his horse, and to help him with Mr. Osborn the alderman with his letters to Constantinople. Sept. 11th, on Tuesday they went to London together, and my wife allso abowt her affayres. Sept. 13th, I writt to Dugenes de Dionigiis to Venys by Mr. John Leonard Haller. Sept.

17th, I writ to the Erle of Osmond. Sept. 29th, Anne cam to my servyse from Mr. Harbert. I payd Mr. Lewys £20, so rest is which I challendg as for my cost and payns for 37 yeres for John his son.

Oct. 12th, I rod to Tundridge. Oct. 13th, I rod from Tundridge to Mr. Coverts at Slawgham. Oct. 15th, I cam home from Slawgham, and dyned at Mr. Holtens, person of Oxstede by Tundridge, a phisitien. Oct. 21st, Jane my wife sowned in the church. Nov. 1st, Mr. Plat, my brother Yong his sonne-in-law, cam to me with a stranger of Trushen, born at Regius Mons: his name is Martinus Faber. The same day cam Mr. Clement the seamaster and Mr. Ingram from Sir George Peckham. Nov. 8th, hayle afternone horam circiter primam: tonitrus circa quartam et sextam. Nov. 9th, Mr. Newbury, who had byn at Cambaya in Inde, cam to me. Nov. 22nd, E. K. went to London, and so the next day conveied by rode toward Blakley, and within ten dayes to returne. Nov. 24th, Saterday night I dremed that I was deade, and afterward my bowels wer taken out I walked and talked with diverse, and among other with the Lord Thresorer who was com to my howse to burn my bokes when I was dead, and thought he loked sourely on me. Dec. 1st, George my man, who had lyne oute all night, this morning used me very dishonestly, and sayd he owed me no servyce. Mr. Bettgran the justice was not at home. Dec. 13th, thunder in the afternone and at sonne-set. Dec. 15th, the 15th day being cownted the 25, 50, 10 dayes ar imagined spent, which have crept in betwene the day of Crist his birth regarding the place of the sonne, and the sonnes place not the 25th day of this month, whiche a civile æquation, but mathematically and religiusly to be substantiated to be for the true term of the periods of annuall revolutions of the sonne sinse the day of Christ his birth.

1583. Jan. 13th, on Sonday the stage at Paris Garden fell down all at ones, being full of people beholding the bearbayting. Many being killed thereby, more hart, and all amased. The godly expownd it as a due plage of God for the wickednes ther usid, and the Sabath day so profanely spent. Jan. 19th, Mr. John Leonard Haller went to London and so to go toward Scotland. Jan. 23rd, the Ryght Honorable Mr. Secretary Walsingham cam to my howse, where by good lok he found Mr. Awdrian Gilbert, and so talk was begonne of Northwest Straights discovery. The Bishop of St. Davyd's (Mr. Middelton) cam to visit me with Mr. Thomas Herbert. The Lord Grey cam to Mr. Secretary, and so they went unto Greenwich (?). Jan. 24th, I, Mr. Awdrian Gilbert, and John Davis went by appointment to Mr. Secretary to Mr. Beale his howse, where onely we four were secret, and we made Mr. Secretarie privie of the N.W. passage, and all charts and rutters were agreed uppon in generall.

Feb. 2nd, Rolandus Dee baptizatus. Feb. 3rd, Mr. Savile, Mr. Powil the yonger, travaylors, Mr. Ottomeen his sonne, cam to be acquaynted with me. Feb. 4th, Mr. Edmunds of the Privie Chamber, Mr. Lee who had byn in Moschovia, cam to be acquaynted with me. Feb. 11th, the Quene lying at Richemond went to Mr. Secretary Walsingham to dynner; she coming by my dore gratiously called me to her, and so I went by her horse side as far as where Mr. Hudson dwelt. Εϱ μαιεστι αξεδ με οβοσκυϱελι οφ μουνσιευϱὶς στατε: διξι βιοθανατος εϱιτ. Roland went with his nurse to her howse to Estshene. Feb. 18th, the Lady Walsingham cam suddenly into my howse very freely, and shortly after that she was gone cam Syr Francys himself and Mr. Dyer. Feb. 24th, Jane churched. Feb. 26th, I delivered my boke to the Lord Threasorer for the correction of the Calender.x

x. This work, although never entirely printed, created much sensation at the time, and was the cause of considerable controversy among the politicians as well as literati. The Memorial on this subject which Dee presented to the Privy Council has been printed by Hearne and others, but it is not generally known that the original manuscript of the actual treatise on the correction of the Calendar is still preserved in Ashmole's library, No. 1789, and is the very book which Dee alludes to above. It is inscribed "to the Right Honorable and my singular good Lorde, the Lorde Burghley, Lorde Threasorer of Englande," with the following verses:—

"Το ὅτι and το διοτι,
I shew the thing and reason why;
At large, in breif, in middle wise,

29

I humbly give a playne advise;
For want of tyme, the tyme untrew
Yf I have myst, commaund anew
Your honor may. So shall you see
That love of truth doth govern me."

The work itself is entitled, "A playne Discourse and humble Advise for our Gratious Queene Elizabeth, her most Excellent Majestie to peruse and consider, as concerning the needful Reformation of the Vulgar Kalender for the civile yeres and daies accompting, or verifyeng, according to the tyme truely spent."

March 6th, I, and Mr. Adrian Gilbert and John Davis, did mete with Mr. Alderman Barnes, Mr. Townson and Mr. Yong and Mr. Hudson, abowt the N.W. voyage. March 17th, Mr. John Davys went to Chelsey with Mr. Adrian Gilbert to Mr. Radforths, and so the 18th day from thence toward Devonshyre. March 18th, Mr. North from Poland, after he had byn with the Quene he cam to me. I receyved salutation from Alaski, Palatine in Poland; salutation by Mr. North who cam before to the Quene, and next to me was his message, hor. 12. Nurse Lydgatt at Estshene was payd for 5 pound candell, 6 pound sope, and the wagis due from Rowland his birth. April 18th, the Quene went from Richemond toward Grenwich, and at her going on horsbak, being new up, she called for me by Mr. Rawly his putting her in mynde, and she sayd "quod defertur non aufertur," and gave me her right hand to kisse. April 24th, nurse was payd for Rowland all her wagis tyll Monday the 22 of this month, 16 pence a weke: she had all her candell and sope before.

May 1st, Albertus Laski, Polonus, Palatinus Scradensis, venit Londinum.*y* May 4th, Mr. Adrian Gilbert and Mr. Pepler went by water to Braynford, and so to ride into Devonshire. May 7th, E. K. went toward London, and so to go homeward for 10 or 12 dayes. Dies Quadragesimus a die Veneris ante Pascham. May 13th, I becam acquaynted with Albertus Laski at 7½ at night, in the Erle of Lecester his chamber in the court at Greenwich. This day was my lease of Devonshyre mynes sealed at Sir Leonell Ducket's hows. May 18th, the Prince Albertus Laski cam to me at Mortlake, with onely two men. He cam at afternone and tarryed supper, and after sone set. Nurse Rowland was payd all tyll the 20th of this month. June 15th, abowt 5 of the clok cam the Polonian Prince Lord Albert Lasky down from Bissham, where he had lodged the night before, being returned from Oxford whither he had gon of purpose to see the universityes, wher he was very honorably used and enterteyned. He had in his company Lord Russell, Sir Philip Sydney, and other gentlemen: he was rowed by the Quene's men, he had the barge covered with the Quene's cloth, the Quene's trumpeters, &c. He cam of purpose to do me honor, for which God be praysed! June 19th, the Lord Albert Laski cam to me and lay at my hows all nyght. Nurse Rowland payd her wagis ending the 17th day of this month.

y. "The year of our Lorde God 1583, the laste daye of Aprill, the Duke or Prince of Vascos in Polonia, came to London and was lodged at Winchester Howse."—MS. Douce, 363, fol. 125. This account differs from Dee's by a single day.

July 1st, Master Mills his answer of no hopes in my sute at Grenewich. July 7th, George was dismissed my servys and payd all reconings in the presens of goodman Hilton and Mistres Kelly in my study. July 10th, Thomas Hoke of Cranford cam to my service, but he went away agayn the 23 day of this month. July 30th, the Quene removed on Tuesday from Greenwich to Sion by water; coming by my dore . . . July 31st, the Quene's gift of 40 angells^z sent by the Erle of Lecester his secretarie Mr. Lloyd, throwgh the Erle his speche to the Quene. Mr. Rawlegh his letter unto me of hir Majesties good disposition unto me. Aug. 1st, John Halton minister dwelling in London with . . . bowed in and looked, and the . . . a Wurcetershire man, a wicked spy cam to my howse, whom I used as an honest man, and found nothing wrong as I thought. I was sent to E.

K. Aug. 7th, Mr. William Burrow passed by me. Aug. 14th, payd nurse Lydgatt for Rowland for two monthes ending the 12th day. Aug. 18th, a great tempest of wynde at mydnyght. Maxima era E. K. cum uxore ejus. Sept. 21st, we went from Mortlake, and so the Lord Albert Lasky, I, Mr. E. Kelly, our wives, my children and familie, we went toward our two ships attending for us, seven or eight myle below Gravessende.

z. "Her Majestie being informed by the Right Honourable Earle of Leicester, that whereas the same day in the morning he had told me that his Honour and Lord Laskey would dine with me within two dayes after, I confessed sincerely unto him that I was not able to prepare them a convenient dinner, unless I should presently sell some of my plate or some of my pewter for it. Whereupon her Majestie sent unto me very royally within one hour after forty angels of gold from Sion, whether her Majestie was now come by water from Greenwich."—Dr. Dee's Compendious Memoriall, p. 511.

1586. July 10th, Mr. William Maynard natus hora 12 noctis, vel paulo post, Londini. Sept. 14th, Trebonam venimus. Oct. 18th, E. K. recessit a Trebona versus Pragam curru delatus; mansit hic per tres hebdomadas. Nov. 8th, illustrissimus princeps versus Pragam; iter institit hora tertia a meridie. Nov. 14th, rescripsi ad Victorem Reinholdum. Nov. 19th, to the glas hows. Nov. 21st, Michael was begone to be weaned. Nov. 22nd, recepi literas Jacobi Memschiti. Dec. 8th, Monday abowt none Mr. Edward Garland cam to Trebona to mee from the Emperor of Moschovia, according to the articles before sent unto me by Thomas Hankinson. Dec. 11th, St. Poloniensis obiit: natus anno 1530 die 13 Januarii, hora quarta mane min. 26, in Transylvania. Obiit, hora secunda post mediam noctem, ut intellexi ex literis D{ni} Lasky, receptis die 29 per Alexandrum. Dec. 19th, 19die (novi kalendarii) ad gratificandum Domino Edouardo Garlando, et Francisco suo fratri, qui Edouardus nuncius mihi missus erat ab Imperatore Moschoviæ ut ad illum venirem, E. K. fecit proleolem lapidis in proportione unius . . . gravi arenæ super quod vulgaris oz. et

½ et producta est optimi auri oz. fere: quod aurum post distribuimus a crucibolo una dedimus Edouardo. Dec. 30th, E. K. versus Pragam.

1587. Jan. 8th, cam Nicolas du Haut, Frenchman of Lorrayn, who had byn lackay to my frende Otho Henrick Duke of Brunswik and Lienburgh, to seke a servyse, being dismissed by passport from his Lord after his long sikenes. Jan. 14th, Doctor Reinholdt of Salfeldt cam to Trebona with Abraham. His sute of the salt. Doctor Reinholdt revisit versus Pragam 20 die. Jan. 18th, rediit E. K. a Praga. E. K. browght with him from the Lord Rosenberg to my wyfe a chayne and juell estemed at 300 duckettes; 200 the juell stones, and 100 the gold. Jan. 21st, E. K. again to Prage and so to Poland ward. Feb. 5th, I tok a jornay of myself from Trebon to Newhowse, two myles of, to mete my Lord to comen with him. I toke two horsemen of the cyty with me. Feb. 9th, Illustriss.[aa] venit a Vienna ad Trebonam. Feb. 12th, ivit Illustriss. versus Crocoviam. Feb. 19th, E. K.[bb] cam from Poland abowt none to Trebone: I sent word to my Lord straight. Feb. 21st, my Lord sending no word yet, I sent another message. March 3rd, a Cremona ad Trebonam. March 7th, E. K. dedit nobis 300 ducata. Recepimus a Domino Illustrissimo 3300. March 9th, iter regium. March 14th, venimus Reichstein. March 17th, reditus a Reichstein. March 21st, E. K. gave me 170 more, and of the 200 for changing 60 remayne. Contumelie et contemptus a Cholek et a Schonberg. March 23rd, venimus Trebonam. March 26th, the Lord Biberstein, comming from Cranbaw from the Lord Rosenberg, passing by Trebona, sent for me to his ynn to make acquayntance with me. E. K. equitavit Crotoviam. April 4th, actio tertia incepit. April 18th, actionis tertiæ finis. May 1st, vidi (doctore meo premonstrante) Michaelium Nuncium non Mersaelem. Laus sit Deo et doctori meo E. K.! June 14th, nuptiæ Domini Thomæ Kelei. June 17th, nsgre guvf shy zbar Vnar unq gurz abg. June 22nd, Mr. Francis Garland went toward England from Trebona.

aa. He frequently speaks of Prince Albert Leski under the title of Illustrissimus.
bb. It is almost unnecessary to observe that these initials refer to Edward Kelly.

July 5th, Sonday, I set the two erthes with theyr water agayn uppon them. July 9th, Mr. Francis Pucci cam and browght Chrisan Franken with him, who, he sayd, had now recanted his wycked boke against Christ, wherof I was glad. Illustrissimus cum Domina venerat Trebona. July 11th, colloquium inter Illustrissimum Dominum, Dominum E. K. et me, a meridie, inter nos tres. July 13th, Francys Pacci recessit. July 19th, a certayn kinde of recommendation between our wives. Next day saw relenting of E. K. also by my Lord's entrety. July 20th, Illustrissimus abiit cum principissa sua versus Cremoniam. Aug. 13th, amice cum Domino Edouardo Keleo de tribus illis votis. Aug. 17th, E. K. cum fratre et Ludovico ... Aug. 18th, we understode how E. K. went to Badwise to bed, and went but this day at none from thence. Aug. 20th, John Basset cam to Trebona. Aug. 23rd, Mr. E. K. cam from Lyntz fayre. Sept. 1st, Tuesday morning, covenanted with John Basset to teach the children the Latyn tong, and I do give him seven duckats by the quarter, and the term to begyne this day; and so I gave him presently seven duckatts Hungary, in gold, before my wife. God spede his work! Sept. 3rd, 4th, continua quasi pluvia per biduum istud. Sept. 4th, Basset his hurlyburly with Mr. T. Kelly. Sept. 16th, the Lord Biberstein cam to Trebon, and Cracht with him. Sept. 22nd, my Lord cum from Crummow to Trebon with my Lady. Sept. 26th, my Lord went toward Prage. Sept. 28th, I delivered to Mr. Ed. Kelley (ernestly requiring it as his part) the half of all the animall which was made. It is to weigh 20 ownces; he wayed it himself in my chamber: he bowght his waights purposely for it. My Lord had spoken to me before for some, but Mr. Kelly had not spoken. Sept. 30th, T. K. and J. C.[cc] went toward Prage.

cc.   That is, Thomas Kelley and John Carp.

Oct. 12th, Mr. E. K. toward Prage on horsbak. Oct. 13th, mane paulo ante ortum solis observavi radio astronomico inter ... et ... gradus 2 minuta prima 22, et erat ... sub Tauro in eadem linea perpendiculari ante oculum demissa super horizonta altitudo erat vix quatuor graduum. Oct. 15th, hyred Nicolas. Oct. 20th, I toke up the furniture for the action. Oct. 26th, Mr. Edward Kelly cam to Trebona from Prage. Oct. 28th and 29th, John Carp did begyn to make furnaces over the gate, and he used of my rownd bricks, and for the yern pot was contented now to use the lesser bricks, 60 to make a furnace. Oct. 31st, Ed. Hilton cam to Trebona in the morning. Nov. 8th, E. K. terribilis expostulatio, accusatio, &c. hora tertia a meridie. Nov. 17th, John Basset had seven ducketts beforehand for his second quarter's wages, begynning the 1st. Nov. 21st, Saterday at night Mr. Francis Garland cam from England to Trebona and browght me a letter from Mr. Dyer and my brother Mr. Richard. Nov. 24th, at the marriag super Critzin the Grand Captayn disdayned to com thither to supper in the Rad howse of Trebona becawse E. K. and I were there; and sayd farder that we wer ... Dec. 1st to 11th, my Lord lay at Trebon and my Lady all this tyme. Dec. 10th, Mr. John Carpio went toward Prage to marry the mayden he had trubbled; for the Emperor's Majestie, by my Lord Rosenberg's means, had so ordred the matter. Dec. 12th, afternone somwhat; Mr. Ed. Keley his lamp overthrow, the spirit of wyne long spent to nere, and the glas being not stayed with buks abowt it, as it was wont to be; and the same glas so flitting on one side, the spirit was spilled out, and burnt all that was on the table where it stode, lynnen and written bokes,—as the bok of Zacharius with the Alkanor that I translated out of French for som by spirituall could not; Rowlaschy his thrid boke of waters philosophicall; the boke called Angelicum Opus, all in pictures of the work from the beginning to the end; the copy of the man of Badwise Conclusions for the Transmution of metalls; and 40 leaves in 4°, intitled, Extractiones Dunstani, which he himself extracted and noted out of Dunstan his boke, and the very boke of Dunstan was but cast on the bed hard by from the table.

1588. Jan. 1st, abowt nine of the clok afternone, Michel, going chilyshly with a sharp stik of eight ynches long and a little wax candell light on the top of it, did fall upon the playn bords in Marie's chamber, and the sharp point of the stik entred throwgh the lid of his left ey toward the corner next the nose, and so persed throwgh, insomuch that great abundance of blud cam out under the lid, in the very corner of the sayd eye; the hole on the owtside is not bygger then a pyn's hed; it was anoynted with St. John's oyle. The boy slept well. God spede the rest of the cure! The next day after it apperid that the first towch of the stikes point was at the very myddle of the apple of the ey, and so (by God's mercy and favor) glanced to the place where it entred; with the strength of his hed and the fire of his fulness, I may make some shew of it to the prayse of God for his mercies and protection. Jan. 11th, Nicolas was sore hart circa 8½ hora nocte. Jan. 13th, at dynner tyme Mr. Edward Kelly sent his brother, Mr. Th. K. to me with these words, "My brother sayth that you study so much, and therfor, seeing it is to late to go to day to Cromlaw, he wisheth you to come to pass the tyme with him at play." I went after dynner and playd, he and I against Mr. F. Gore and Mr. Rob tyll supper tyme, in his dynyng rome: and after supper he cam and the others, and we playd there two or three howres, and frendely departed. This was then after the great and wonderful unkindnes used toward me in taking my man. Jan. 14th, Mr. Edward Kelly rid to Crumlow, being sent for by my Lord. I receyved a letter from the Lord Chamberlain. Jan. 18th, Mistres Lidda K. had an abortion of a girle of 5 or 6 monthes; she was mery and well till the night before; I helped to finde the dead birthe within one howr after I had caused her to have myrh given unto her in wyne warmed, the quarter of a ounce; better after she was discharged of the secondyne, and all at ones. The woman was sufficiently strong after. Jan. 19th, Mr. E. K. cam from Crumlow. Feb. 4th, Mr. Francys Garland and his brother Robert went from Trebona to go toward England: I wrote to Mr. Dyer and Mr. Yonge. Feb. 8th, Mr. E. K. at nine of the clok afternone sent for me to his laboratory over the gate to se how he distilled sericon, according as in tyme past and of late he hard of me out of Riplay. God lend his hart to all charity and virtue! Feb. 16th, John Carpe cam to Trebon after his marriage. Feb. 19th, Mr. E. K. did qvfpybfr fbz, nppbhagrq zl seraqrf, ubj hageh gurl jre. Feb. 28th, mane paulo ante ortum solis natus est Theodoras Trebonianus Dee, ascendente Sirio in horoscopo, die dominica. March 1st, baptisatus erat Theodoras Dee Trebonæ ante meridiem. March 6th, I went to Newhous and dyned at the castell. March 12th, my Lord cam to Trebona and my Lady. March 24th, Mr. K. put the glas in dung. March 26th, my Lord sent one of his secretaries with answer to my letter, and with offer and promys of all where he can pleasure me, circa 5 post meridiem. March 29th, my Lord and Lady from Trebon toward Crumlow. The midwife's husbond's name of Newhowse is David Peregrinus, perhaps of the familie of Petrus Peregrinus, otherwise called Peter of Maharncourt, of Picardy.

April 3rd, Mr. Pucci disquietted Mr. E. K. abowt requesting an action, to which he had one of our six monthes actions, being now the term begynning the fourth day of this month. The ende of our talke was a strange spech of Mr. Kelly to Fr. Puccy. After 15 wekes write to me, and I will answer you. April 6th, Edmond Hilton went from Trebona toward Prage with Mr. John Carpe, and so toward England. April 10th, I writ to Mr. Edward Kelly and to Mistres Kelly ij. charitable letters, requiring at theyr hands mutual charity. I went to Mr. Captain Chritzin, to know if he were offended to me, who in outward shew used me reasonably curteously. April 12th, my wife churched, and we receyved the communion. John Carpe browght his wife from Prage to Trebona. April 17th, Doctor Reinholt cam to Trebona. April 22nd, nocte hora 9 terribilis et falsa accusatio vel suspicio, quod Puccia annunciavit contra D. K. et ipsum principia (?). May 1st, Mr. Carpio rid to my Lord to the holy well at the glass hows, four myles from Trebona, with my letters of purgation for Puccies his attempts or intents in his letters to my bond and Mr. Kelly, unknown to me. May 4th, Mr. Carpio browght me word of my Lord's displeasure, conveyed and confirmed by cozen Pully his letters. Deus ille sit propitius! May 7th, post afflictionem magnam meam, mei misertus est Deus! Puccia, die eodem venerunt literæ Principis ad Dominum E. K., quæ dies declarabat amici sui infamum meum ne dignitatem: sed non reddebatur nisi, valde præfex, valde erat ingratæ ille literæ ipsi Domino E. K. Misericordia Dei magna! Omne quod vivit laudet Deum! Hæc est dies quam fecit Dominus! May 10th, E. K. did open the great secret to me, God be thanked! May 19th, hora 10 cum circumstantiis necessariis. May 22nd, Mistris Kelly received the sacrament, and to me and my wife gave her hand in charity; and we rushed not from her. May 30th, Michael was sik of an ague, and Mr. Kelly likewise. June 4th, the howses burnt at Trebon in the morning early on Whitsonday. June 8th, Illustrissimus venit Trebonam. June 11th, Illustrissimus recessit in Dominica a Trebona versus Pragam. My Lord sent Critzin with his compliments unto me, and to offer me help, hora prima a meridie. A letter cam from T. G. of Mr. Dyer, his being three myle from Trebona, but it was not so. Mr. Dier sent word by Francis Garland wher. June 13th, cam Francis Garland and Mr. Edmond Cooper, brother to Mistris Kelly, to Trebona. June 16th, Francis Garland went to fynde and bring Mr. Dier. June 19th, I had a grudging of the ague. June 22nd, I did evydently receive the ague, and layd down.

July 7th, Mr. Thomas Sowthwell cam to Trebona to visit us. July 17th, Mr. Thomas Sowthwell of his own courteous nature did labor with Mr. Edmond Cowper and indirectly with Mistres Kelly for to furder charity and frendship among us. July 20th, Mr. Dier cam to Trebona, July 22nd, a meridie circa 10 Mr. Edward διερ διδ ινιυριε με υνκινδελε. July 23rd, reconciliatio bona cum Magistro διερ υυιθ υυυρδς . . . φακτο μεδιαντε E. K. Aug. 1st, Mr. Harry Maynard natus nocte circa horam 11 Mortlak. Aug. 4th, Illustrissimus cam from Crachovia to Trebon, and there on Friday before dynner cam up Mr. Dyer, who lay in my chamber, and entertayned him honorably. Aug. 5th, after dynner the little boy, sonne to the Captayn of Rhaudnitz, hurt Arthur's nose with a raser, not in anger but by chance wantonly. Aug. 6th, my Lord and Lady went toward Prage. Aug. 7th, this day I covenanted and hyred John Hammond, jentleman, to serve me in his honest servyces for one yere, and to have 30 dolers for his full and all manner of wages. Aug. 9th, Tuesday, Mr. Dyer went from Trebon, having in company Mr. Edmond Cowper, Francys Garland, and his man Rowley. Aug. 13th, Mr. Thomas Sowthwell ryd to Prag ward from Trebon. He told us of the philosopher (his scholemaster to write) whose name was Mr. Swyft, who gave him a lump of the philosopher's stone so big as his fist: a Jesuit named Mr. Stale had it of him. Aug. 14th, Mr. Sowthwell cam againe. Aug. 24th, vidi divinam aquam demonstratione magnifici domini et amici mei incomparabilis D. Ed. Kelei ante meridiem tertia hora. Aug. 27th, John Basset (so namyng himself) otherwise truely named Edward Whitlok, under pretence of going to Budweiss to buy cullors and so to return agayn, did convey himselfe from my servyce of teaching Arthur grammer. Sept. 3rd, my lord and lady cam to Trebon. Sept. 12th, spes confirmata. Sept. 15th, the Lord Chamberlain cam to Trebona, and went away on the 17th. The rancor and dissimulation now evident to me, God deliver me! I was not sent for.

Oct. 17th, Mystres Kelly and the rest rode toward Punchartz in the morning. Oct. 18th, my Lord and my Lady ryd toward Ctumnate. Oct. 25th, Mr. Ed. Kelley and John Carpio rode toward Prage: this night to Wesely, two myles. Nov. 5th, I dreamed that the toth next my top toth skarse cold hang in my hed, the toth on the right side above. Nov. 6th, Mr. Kelly cam home from Prage and Mr. Francys Garland, and Edward Rolls with him from Eglis. Nov. 15th, in the fornone, snow and close clowdy. Nov. 16th, the Lord and Lady Rosenberg cam from Crummedo to Trebon in the evening. Nov. 20th, this Sunday before dynner the Lord and Lady Rosenberg went from Trebon toward Prage. Nov. 23rd, Mr. Francis Garland and Edward Rowly, Mr. Dyer his servant, went from Trebon toward England. I writ to the Quene's Majestie, Mr. Dyer, Mr. Yong, and Edward Hilton. Dec. 4th, I gave to Mr. Ed. Kelley my Glass, so highly and long estemed of our Quene, and the Emperor Randolph the second, de quo in præfatione Euclidis fit mentio.[dd] The letter of 500,000 ducats required. Dec. 7th, γρεατ φρενδκιπ προμισιδ φορ μανι, ανδ τυυο ουνκες οφ θε θινγ. Dec. 13th, Mr. Edward Kelley gave me the water, erth and all. Dec. 14th, Edmond Hilton cam again to Trebon from England. Dec. 18th, I did understand by Mr. Kelley that my glass which he had given to my Lord Rosenberg, the Lord Rosenberg had given it to the Emperor. Dec. 23rd, I went to the new made citie Kaiser Radnef Stadt, by Budneis, to ovirsee what Joachim Reimer had done abowt my coaches making. Radulphus Sagiensis Gallus Normannus, venit Trebonam, chimiæ et naturalis magiæ studiosus.

dd. This refers to the earliest English translation of Euclid by Billingsley, which was published in 1570, with a long preface by Dr. Dee. Professor De Morgan is of opinion that the translation also was by Dee, or that Billingsley may have been only a pupil who worked immediately under his directions. The passage to which Dee alludes is as follows:—"a man to be curstly affrayed of his owne shadow; yea, so much to feare, that if you, being alone nere a certaine glasse, and proffer, with dagger or sword, to foyne at the glasse, you shall suddenly be moved to give backe (in maner) by reason of an image appearing in the ayre betwene you and the glasse with like hand, sword, or dagger, and with like quicknes, foyning at your very eye, likewise as you do at the glasse. Straunge this is to heare of, but more mervailous to behold then these my wordes cam signifie; and neverthelesse by demonstration opticall the order and cause therof is certified; even so, as the effect is consequent." I refer the reader also to Mr. Barlow's History of Optics in the Encyclopedia Metropolitana.

1589. Jan. 3rd, Rudolphus Sagiensis Normannus recessit versus Pragam. Jan. 17th, the humming in my eares began. Jan. 19th, circa undecimam noctis abortiebatur Domina Lydda uxor D. Thomæ Kelly ex duobus masculis vix sex mensium, et anno precedente hoc ejusdem uxor abortiebatur puella. Jan. 20th, Mr. Kelly showed me the Lord Rosenberg his letter; when he wrot that of me he hard no more of my going hens, and if Menschik hath not performed as he willed him, that if I send him word he will so dispatch me that therby I shall not nede to stay here, as he had confidently heretofore warned Mr. Kelley, so now he did request him to take leve of me at my departure. And then Mr. Kelly did loke and truly confess that my . . . Jan. 25th, Mr. Mains cam to visit us; the Erle of

Schwiczenbagh thre sones. Jan. 31st, Tuesday, I sent Edmond Hilton to Prage, and Zacharias Mathias of Buelweiss, to buy 10 or 12 coach horses and saddell horses for 300 dollers. Feb. 4th, I delivered to Mr. Kelley the powder, the bokes, the glas and the bone, for the Lord Rosenberg; and he thereuppon gave me dischardg in writing of his own hand subscribed and sealed. Feb. 12th, Edmond Hilton cam from Prage with nine Hungarian horses bowght toward our jornay. Feb. 16th, Mr. Edward Kelley rode toward Prage after none, John Carpio, Edmond Hilton, Henry Garlande, Thomas Simkinson, Lodovik. March 11th, from Trebon in Bohemia. March 18th, to Nuremberg. March 20th, from Nuremberg. March 26th, to Frankfurt on the Mane.

April 19th, to Breme. May 1st, Katharin by a blow on the eare given by her mother did bled at the nose very much, which did stay for an howre and more; afterward she did walk into the town with nurse; upon her coming home she bled agayn. May 11th, John of Gloles cam to Breme. May 13th, I cam to lie at my hyred hows. May 17th, the three saddle horse put to grass to the town meddowes for nine ducets tyll Mychelmas. May 21st, the Landgrave of Hesse his letters to me and the city of Breme. May 25th, I sent the Lantgrave my twelve Hungarish horses. June 2rd and 13th, Mr. Duerend and Mr. Hart went toward Stade. They had scaped from the Spanish servise in Flanders with Syr William Stanley. June 6th, Dr. Kenrich Khanradt of Hamburgh visitted me. Mr. Thomas Kelly his wife, Francis Garland, Rolls, from Standen toward England. June 16th, Edmund Hilton toward Prage. June 19th, Hans of Glotz went toward Standen, and so toward England. June 23rd, Mr. Daniel van der Multon cam to me. Ultima die mensis istius circa meridiem maximi imbres, tonitrua, grandines.

July 6th, Thursday the 26th of June (by the old accownt and the 6th of July by new accownt) Mr. Hart, the minister of the English company, and Mr . . . the governor's deputy of the English company at Stade, did visit me at my howse in Breme. July 18th, Mr. Yong and Mr. Secretary his letter. July 30th, Edmond Hilton cam from Prage to Breme by Stade. Aug.

2nd, veteri stilo, the nyght following, my terrible dream that Mr. Kelly wold by force bereave me of my bokes, toward daybreak. Aug. 5th, novo stylo, Edmond Hilton went toward Stade, to go toward England, with my letters to disclose the treason of Perkins. Ther went in this company two English people, Mr. Rolous Tattin and George Losin. Aug. 7th, the first of the seven half fasts. Aug. 14th, Theodor wened. Aug. 21st, John Hammond to Stade. Aug. 22nd, natus William Hazilwood mane hora sexta fere, forte hora 5 min. 45, by Maydston in Kent. Sept. 9th, Roger his serviceable letters of the Lord Rosenberg. Sept. 12th, the wynde cam East after five wekes most part West. Sept. 16th, ante meridiem hora 9 in delinquiciis A. C. incidi ex ingratitudine concepta ex verbis uxoris, et Anallæ Mariæ. Sept. 22nd, stilo veteri, I delivered to Mr. Jacob for England by Embden my letters.

Oct. 3rd, D. Witischindi his hard dealings with me: he bad Mr. Harper the Secretary to give me warning of my howse. Oct. 9th, warned out of my howse hora prima a meridie. Oct. 14th, John Hanward gave me warning that he desyred to go travayle toward Italy; but first to Master Kelly of whome he hoped to have good help. Oct. 17th, Mr. Sowthwell and Mr. Gawyne Smyth cam to me to Bream. Oct. 23rd, Mr. Sowthwell and Mr. Smyth went from Bream. Oct. 29th, Wenefrida Goose inter 9 et 10 a meridie. Oct 31st, letters sent to Stade for Gerwein Greven for her Majestie, Mr. Yong, and Mr. Dyer. Nov. 1st, newes of Mr. Dyer sent ambassador to Denmarke. Nov. 3rd, stilo veteri, I resolved to go into England, hoping to mete Mr. Edward Kelly at Stade, going also into England; and that I suspected uppon Mr. Secretary Walsingham his letters. Nov. 13th, Edmond Hilton and his brother from England, and John a Glotz. Nov. 17th, die lunæ, I met Mr. Dyer comming to Stade, even in the myddle of the town. Nov. 18th, Edmond to Stade ward. Nov. 19th, toke ship by the Vineyard. Dec. 2nd, we cam into the Tems to Gravesende. Dec. 3rd, from the ship to Stratford to Mr. Yong's howse. Dec. 19th, at Richemond with the Queene's Majestie.[cc] Dec. 20th, agreed for my howse with Nicolas Fromonds to occupy as a tenant with better order. Dec. 25th, I lay this night first at my howse. Dec. 29th, Mr. Adrian Gilbert cam to me to Mortlak, and offred me as much as I could require at his hands, both for my goods carryed away, and for the mynes.

ee. Where, according to Aubrey, who received his information from Lilly, he was very favourably received by her Majesty.

1590. Jan. 15th, a terrible tempest of wind, South by West. Jan. 23rd, Mr. Thomas Kelly cam from Brainford; put me in good hope of Sir Edward Kelly his returning: offered me the loane of ten pownds in gold, and afterward sent it me in Hungary new ducketes by John Croker, the same evening. Jan. 26th, I writt to Mr. Adrian Gilbert two letters. I resolved of the order to be offred for agreement with Nicholas Fromonds for my howse and goodes. The 5th of March (by old accownt) was Madinia Newton, my daughter, christened at Mortlak; godfather, Sir George Cary; godmothers, the Lady Cobham and the Lady Walsingham. March 12th, Mrs. Anne Deny born betweene 8 and 9 afternoone. March 14th, Mr. Dyer cam home from Stade. March 17th, Sir Edward Kelly his letter by Francis Garland. March 21st, Sir George Gary cam to Mortlak. March 27th, Jane apprehended hora quinta a meridie.[ff] My children at this Lady Day in Lent, began to go to schole at Mortlak with the scholemaster Mr. Lee: I gave him his howse-rent and forty shillings yerely for my three sons and my daughter. The howse-rent was allmost 4s. yerely of Mr. Fisher his new howse. April 7th, John Spenser cam to me, from Venys new returned, and told me of the Venetian philosopher and the goodnes of his gold. April 16th, good Sir Francis Walsingham died at night hora undecima. April 19th, I delivered my letters to Mr. Thomas Kelley for his brother Sir Edward Kelley, knight, at the Emperor's court at Prage. Francys Garland was by, and Mr. Thomas Kelley his wife. God send them well thither and hither agayn! Mr. Emery had disbursed to me frankly betwene the tyme from Shrovetyde tyll this May £25. May 5th, Mr. Thomas Jack restored unto me part of my magnes stone. May

8th, I received 20 mark from Sir Richard Lagney, of Longlernay. May 16th, I gave Mr. Lee the scholemaster *5s.* in part of wages. May 18th, the two gentlemen, the unckle Mr. Richard Candish, and his nephew the most famous Mr. Thomas Candish,gg who had sayled rownd abowt the world, did viset me at Mortlake. May 20th, after dynner, I with my brother, Mr. Justice Yong, went to the Archebishop of Canterbury to Lambeth, abowt the personagis who used me well. May 21st, I showed my indignation against Bacchus feast at Braynferd intended; gave the Bishop of London warning, who toke it in very good part. Katharyne, my dowghter, was put to Mistres Brayce at Braynferd, hir mother and Arthur went with her after dynner. May 23rd, I lent to goodman Dalton, the carpenter, xxs. for a month. May 29th, 30th, bona nova de industria Domini Richardi Candishii, cum Regina et Archiepiscopo et Domino Georgio Carey, de propositione Etonensis Collegii obtinendi legem. He sent me a hogshed of claret wyne as a gyft. The Lady Cobham sent my wyfe suger and pepper, &c. June 2nd, I writ to Syr Edward Kelly by Mr. William Fowler, merchant, dwelling by Ledenhall. June 3rd, I was very sik uppon two or thre sage leaves eten in the morning; better suddenly at night; when I cast them up, I was well. The pump taken out and the well skoured. June 5th, Thomas Hankinson and Antony my man cam from beyond the seas to Mortlak. June 5th, terrible yll newes of Edward Kelly against me. June 24th, £20 of Mr. Candish by Edward Hilton. June 28th, I payd Mr. Hudson for all his corn, and also for the wood tyll May, receyved synce I cam home.

ff. There are a great many brief notices in this diary relative to Jane Dee, most of which are expressed in astrological symbols; and as they are exceedingly difficult to decipher satisfactorily, and are certainly of very little, if any importance, I have thought it expedient to omit them. The entry of "Vnar unq gurz" is also of frequent occurrence, though what "gurz" can refer to I have not been able to discover.

gg. Dee has preserved several interesting notices of his intimacies with the principal navigators of his time. A general reference to Hackluyt will be sufficient.

July 6th, Mr. Stockden was all payd for his wood 40s. I gave the scholemaster Mr. Lee 5s. in part of wagis: he browght me my hammer from Mr. Jak, so he hath a quarter's wagis 10s. July 8th, I receyved Sir Edward Kelly his letters, dated at Prage the 24th of May stylo novo. No mention is made of his brother Mr. Thomas Kelly coming over. July 10th, the executor of the Lady Ducket requered the det. July 11th, I payd nurse Barwik 12s. for ii. monthis wagis for Madinia: so she is payd for five monthes.

July 13th, I went to the Archbishop of Canterbury: talked with him boldly of my right to the personages, and to the treatise of Sir Edward Kelley his Alchimy. July 14th, Mr. Gawayn Smyth spake frendely for me to the Quene, and she disclosed her favor toward me. July 16th, my mynde was somewhat bent to deale with my alchimicall exercises. July 25th, I writ a letter of thanks to the Lord Threasorer by Edmond Hilton. I sent the Lord Chancellor his letters from Brunswyk, of Conrad Nettlebronner his ill behaviour. July 31st, I gave Mr. Richard Candish the copy of Paracelsus twelve lettres, written in French with my own hand; and he promised me, before my wife, never to disclose to any that he hath it; and that yf he dye before me he will restore it agayn to me; but if I dy befor him, that he shall deliver it to one of my sonnes, most fit among them to have it. Theoddor had a sore fall on his mowth at mid-day. Aug. 2nd, Mrs. Stoner's sonne born circa horam tertiam a meridie. Nurs her great affliction of mynde. Aug. 5th, Rowland fell into the Tems over hed and eares abowt noone or somewhat after. Aug. 8th, I gave Nurse Barwick six shillings, so she is payd for the half yere due on Weynsday next. Aug. 9th, I payd to Mr. Lee the scholemaster 5s. Aug. 22nd, Ann my nurse had long byn tempted by a wycked spirit: but this day it was evident how she was possessed of him. God is, hath byn, and shall be her protector and deliverer! Amen.

Aug. 25th, Anne Frank was sorowfol, well comforted and stayed in God's mercyes acknowledging. Aug. 26th, at night I anoynted (in the name of Jesus) Ann Frank her brest with the holy oyle. Aug. 30th, in the morning she required to be anoynted, and I did very devowtly prepare myself, and pray for vertue and powr and Christ his blessing of the oyle to the expulsion of the wycked; and then twyse anoynted, the wycked one did resest a while. Sept. 1st, I receyved letters from Sir Edward Kelley by Francis Garland. Sept. 8th, Nurse Anne Frank wold have drowned hirself in my well, but by divine Providence I cam to take her up befor she was overcome of the water. Sept. 23rd, Sonday, I gave Nurse Barwyk six shillings for a monthis wages to ende on Wensday comme a fortnight; Mrs. Stackden was by. Sept. 29th, Nurse Anne Frank most miserably did cut her owne throte, afternone abowt four of the clok, pretending to be in prayer before her keeper, and suddenly and very quickly rising from prayer, and going toward her chamber, as the mayden her keper thowght, but indede straight way down the stayrs into the hall of the other howse, behinde the doore, did that horrible act; and the mayden who wayted on her at the stayr-fote followed, her, and missed to fynde her in three or fowr places, tyll at length she hard her rattle in her owne blud.

Oct. 11th, Mr. Cumber cam to me. Oct. 14th, payd Nurse Barwik six shillings for one month ending on the seventh, being Wensday. Oct. 15th, this afternoone and all the night following a great storme of wynde at North-West. One Prychard that had marryed Proctor Lewes his widdow, demaunded £24 of me uppon an obligation of £64: whereof by the very note on the bak of the same £48 is payd, so that £16 only remayne and not £24, as he unduely demanded: which £16 I challenged for the costes of his sonne John, three yeres and longer being with me in Mortlak, and having also his lerning free. Notwithstanding my wife afraid payd a pownd or two to Mr. Lewys of that £16, and yet Prichard will go to law. Nov. 12th, the Archbishop of Canterbury gave me £5 in ryalls and angels circa horam decimam matutina. Nov. 20th, Her Majestie cam to Richemond. Nov. 27th, the Quene's Majestie, being at Richemont, graciously sent for me. I cam to her at three quarters of the clok afternone, and she sayd she wold send me something to kepe Christmas with. Nov. 28th, Mr. Candish on Saterday gave my wife forty shillings, and on Tuesday after sent £10 in ryalls and angels, and before he sent me £20, £32 in all. My cousin Mr. Thomas Junes cam in the ende of the terme about St. Andrew's even. Dec. 1st, Her Majestie commaunded Mr. John Herbert, Master of Requests, to write to the Commissioners in my behalf. Dec. 2nd, order taken by the Commissioners for my howse and goods. Her Majesty told Mr. Candish that she wold send me an hundred angels to kepe my Christmas withall. Dec. 3rd, goodwife Tyndale payd for Antony his lodging for eleven wekes dew at his going away *5s. 6d.*, and before she had for seven wekes. Dec. 4th, the Quene's Majestie called for me at my dore circa 3½ a meridie as she passed by, and I met her at Estshene gate, where she graciously, putting down her mask, did say with mery chere, "I thank thee, Dee; there was never promisse made but it was broken or kept." I understode her Majesty to mean of the hundred angels she promised to have sent me this day, as she yester-night told Mr. Richard Candish. Dec. 6th, Mr. Thomas Griffith my cosen from Llanbeder cam to see me, and lay all night with me, and allso Mr. Thomas Jones, and in the Monday morning went by water to London, and so the same day homeward. A meridie circa 3^a recepi a Regina Domina £50. Dec. 8th, at Chelsey disputing with Doctor Mather, bishop of Bristow; in danger of water hora 5½ I stayed at Chelsey. Dec. 14th, the Quene's Majestie called for me at my dore as she rod by to take ayre, and I met her at Estshene gate. Dec. 16th, Mr. Candish receyved from the Quene's Majestie warrant by word of mowth to assure me to do what I wold in philosophie and alchimie, and none shold chek, controll, or molest me; and she sayd that she wold ere long send me £50 more to make up the hundred pound. I gave Mr. Candish the Bishop of Scotland his conclusion with marchaunts. Mr. Candish went from Mortlak at four of clok at nyght toward London and so into Suffolk. Dec. 18th, Mr. Robert Maynard natus circa horam decimam antei meridiem Londini.

1591. Jan. 21st, utterly put owt of hope for recovering the two parsonages[hh] by the Lord Archbishop and the Lord Threasorer. Feb. 13th, Bartilmew cam up. March 2th, borrowed £20 uppon plate and payd this day £19 in Mortlak. March 21st, remember that on Passion Sunday, being the 21st of March by our accownt, all things was payd for to Mr. Thomas Hudson for wood and corne, abowt £14, at his howse when he was syk of the strangury. Allso to godman Bedell was payd £4 for billet, baven, and lose fagot the same day. Payd likewise to gudwife Wesder eight shillings for one monthes nursing of Madinia, and 4s. more beforehande. March 26th, Mr. Beale sent me home the first my own hand copy of the volume of Famous and Rich Discoveries[ii] which I had given anno 1583 to Andrew Strange.

hh. See the "Compendious Rehearsall," published by Hearne from a Manuscript in the Cottonian collection, now partially destroyed by fire, for a more extended account of this.
ii. Now in the Cottonian collection. Ashmole has preserved a copy of it in MS. Ashm. 1790.

May 12th, I payd goodwife Welder xijs. for vij. wekes ending then next from the Wensday before Ester-day last. May 25th, of the old Kalander, Sir Thomas Jones Knight (unaxed) offred me his castell of Emlyn in Wales to dwell in so long as he had any interest in it, whose lease dureth yet twelve yeres, freely, with commodityes adjoining unto it; and allso to have as much mow land for rent, as myght pleasure me sufficiently. The 27th day he confirmed the same his offer agayn before Mr. John Harbert, Master of the Requestes, in his hall in Mortlak; which his offers I did accept of, and he was glad thereof. May 31st, Bartilmew [Hickman] cam up and browght Jane his dowghter with him. Mr. R. Ed. his boke and letter. June 8th, William Aspland of Essex and Th. Collen. June 12th, lent Chronica Hollandiæ Magna to Mr. Beale on Saterday manuscript, which Mr. Webb lent me. June 14th, Jane Hikman to goodwife Tyndall's to lern.

June 27th, Arthur wownded on his hed by his own wanton throwing of a brik-bat upright, and not well avoyding the fall of it agayn, at Mr. Harberts abowt sonn-setting. The half-brik weighed 2½ lb. June 30, Madinia was taken home from goodwife Welder.

July 28th, Mr. Dyer sent me xx. angels by Mr. Thomas Webbes. July 30th, reconciliation betweene Mr. Dyer and me solemnized the afternone on Friday, and on Saterday (the 31st) all day tyll my going by boat at Mr. Webb's lodging at Rochester Howse. July 31st, by old Kalender, abowt an eleven of the clok Jane was at London very faynt syke, redy to swownd, and in a faynt swete. It was thowght that then she quickened. The last of Julie, Saterday by the old accownt, Barthelmew cam up; he went down on Tuesday, the 3rd day of August, from Mortlak. Aug. 2nd, Monday, Mr. William Diggs his philosophicall curtesy all day. Sept. 22nd, Madinia fell from the bed and hurt her forhed abowt one of the clok afternone. Oct. 15th, after midnight very wyndy northerly. Oct. 23rd, a storm of wynde S.W. afternone. Dec. 3rd, wyndie S.W. Dec. 14th, I had a very jentle answer at the Lord Thresorer's hand hora decima ante meridiem at the court of Whitehall. Dec. 20th, a jentle answer of the Lord Threasorer that the Quene wold have me have something at this promotion of bishops at hand.

1592. Jan. 1st, my dowghter Francys borne on New Yeres day at the sun-rising exactly. Jan. 2nd, Barthilmew and his brother Ambrose cam this Sonday to Mortlak. Jan. 9th, Francys christened afternone. Francys went with her nurse to Barne Elms. Mr. Edward Maynard borne in the morning betwene 2 and 3 after mydnight. Arthur fell into a quotidian jentle ague at 9 of the clok in the morning as he was at the servyce in the hall. Jan. 24th, Mr. Thomas Oliver becam acquaynted with me at Mortlak. March 6th, the Quene granted my sute to Dr. Awbrey. March 9th, the pryvy seale at night. March 16th, the great seale. March 18th, Arthur and Katharine were let blud at London by Doctor Dodding's cownsayle. March 24th, £25 Mr. Tho. Mownson. March 25th, I payd £10 to Nicholas Fromonds paulo ante solis occasum, when he most abhominably revyled me. March 30th, on Thursday Mr. Saunders of Ewell sent home my great sea cumpas, but without a nedle; it cam in the night by water.

April 5th, the Lady Russell robbed a little after mydnight of perles, diamands, &c. One John Smyth is suspected, a yong man of thirty yeres old, very ingenious in many handyworkes, melancholek. April 8th, Richard cam to my servyce, 40s. yerely and a livery. April 9th, 10th, agreed with my brother Nicholas Fromonds with Mr. Webbs, at 8 of the clok on Wensday night, and 8 on Tuesday night. April 14th, Winifrede Goose, wife of goodman Goose of Tuddington, dowghter of Harry Wyse, eviley tempted, cam to me with her sister. April 16th, δε θεσαυρο α βοκ. April 27th, filius Mariæ Nevell hora 3½ a meridie et aliquantus tardus by Chichester. May 3rd, Wensday, at 10 of the clok Arthur was put to Westmynster Schole under Mr. Grant and Mr. Camden. May 11th, I borowed ten pound of Master Thomas Smith to be paid at Christmas next. May 12th, great wynde at north. May 15th, Marian cam again a meridie hora septima. May 16th, I rode to Harfelde to the Lord Anderson, Lord Justice of the Common Pleas, 12 myles off. May 25th, hora sexta a meridie mowght have byn a quarell betwene Mr. Web and Mr. Morgan with one eye for £4. left unpayd uppon a bill. June 16th, Sir John Perrot judged to be drawn, hanged, and quartered.

July 23rd, at Grenwich abowt mydnight following this day began the first evydent shew of my grief of kidneys; whereuppon Doctor Giffard caused me to have a glyster, and so the next day I was easid of my grief. July 29th, Robert Theneth of Rushmer by Ypswych made acquaintance with me: he told me of Mr. Carter a man of 80 yeres old in Yorkshyre. Aug. 6th, I went to Nonsuch to the court, wyder the Countess of Warwik sent me word by Mr. Ferdinando of the Quene's gratious speches at St. Crosses, and the Lord Archbishop told me the like. Aug. 8th, after the midnight of Monday, being the 7th day, the second fytt of the stone in my kydnes did molest me for 6 or 7 howres. Aug. 9th, the Lord Threasorer invited me to dynner at Mr. Maynards at Mortlak, where Sir Robert Cecill and Sir Thomas Cisell and his lady wer allso. The Lord Threasorer allso sent me some venison to supper. He invited me to dynner allso the tenth day, where the Lord Cobham cam also to dynner, and after dynner he requested the Lord Threasorer to help me to St. Crosses, which he promised to do his best in. Aug. 11th, Mr. Kemp of Micheam, my old acquayntance, abowt an eleven of clok (allmost) before none, told me of the rare appearing. Aug. 17th, I went to Micheam to Mr. Kemp. Aug. 21st, I went to the Lord Cobham and the Lady Cobham to London. Aug. 23rd, Mr. Cholmely and his mayde ante meridiem hor. 11½. The humor so suddenly falling into the calf of my left leg as if a stone had hit me. Aug. 26th, Mr. Heriot 40*s*.[kk] Auditor Hill, £4. Remember all thing is payd to our nurse at Barnes for the girle Francys Dee from hir birth untyll the ende of her eight month, lacking 12*s*., and on Sunday, the 27th of this August, we so concluded, when we gave the nurse ten shillings. The eight month ended (from Newyere's day morning last) the 12th of this month. Sept. 4th, 5th, 6th, very tempestuous, windy at West, Sowtherly. Sept. 5th, the Tems very shallow at London. Sept. 6th, goodman Warryn of Marketharborogh. Robert Web cam from Mr. Ponsoys to write, and is to com agayn within thre wekes. Sept. 7th, Robert Charles of Northamptonchyre and goodman Warren of Marketharborow in my howse at Mortlak promised me to help Barthilmew Hikman with £12 to pay on Michelmas Day next to discharge the bond for his brother-in-law. This they promised uppon condition I wold be bownd to them to see them repayd agayn. I sent a letter to Sir Robert Thaneth to Rushmer by Ypswych by the wagonman who is at ynn at the George in Lombard Streete. He sayd that Robert Thaneth was at home and well. Sept. 19th, I had on the Sunday abowt 7 of the clok afternone the cramp most extremely in the very centre of the calves of both my legs, and in the place where I had the suddeyn grief on Bartilmew-even last I had payn so intollerable as yf the vaynes or artheries wold have broken by extreme stretching, or how els I cannot tell. The payn lasted abowt half a quarter of an howr. I toke my purgation of six grayns. I began in the morning to drink the drink for the stone in the kydney. Sept. 28th, Mr. Laiesley promised me ten shepe and four quarters of wheat. Sept. 30th, Elizabeth Denby went from me to Mistres Herberts' to servyce.

kk.   This entry is not very clear. It either refers perhaps to Harriot, the celebrated mathematician, or to the London goldsmith whom the Abbotsford novelist has immortalized.

Oct. 13th, I exhibited to the Archbishop of Canterbury two bokes of blasphemie against Christ and the Holy Ghoste, desyring him to cause them to be confuted: one was Christian Franken, printed anno 1585 in Poland; the other was of one Sombius against one Carolius, printed at Ingolstad anno 1582 in octavo. Oct. 14th, 15th, a mighty wynde at sowth-west. Oct. 30th, 31st, one of these two dayes I hurt my left shyn against the sharp small end of a wooden rammar abowt four of the clok afternone. Nov. 1st, Mr. Ashly, his wife, and their familie, did com to my howse and remayned ther. They had my mother's chamber, the mayde's chamber, and all the other howse. Nov. 9th, Her Majestie's grant of my supplication for commissioners to comme to me. The Lady Warwik obteyned it. Nov. 22nd, the commissioners from Her Majestie, Mr. Secretary Wolly and Sir Thomas George, cam to Mortlak to my howse. Nov. 28th, to Richard Walkdyne of his wagis 20*s*. Dec. 1st, a little after none the very vertuous Cowntess of Warwik sent me word very speedily by hir gentleman Mr. Jones from the cowrt at Hampton Cowrt that this day Her Majestie had granted to send me spedily an hundred marks, and that Sir Thomas George had very honorably dealt for me in the cause. Dec. 2nd, Sir Thomas George browght me a hundred marks from her Majestie. Dec. 24th to 31st, at Mr. Lurensey of Tooting all these days, and Newyere's Day allso, and so cam home by coach (as we went) by Tuesday none, I, my wyfe, Arthur, Kate, &c. Dec. 31st, at Tooting at Mr. R. Luresey his howse; abowt thre of the clok after dynner dyd the Bishop of Laigham serve process uppon me for the nangle, but most unduely.

1593. January, the Lord Threasorer lay dangerously syk in the begynning of this month. Jan. 2nd, I cam home from Tooting. Jan. 7th, I receyved letters from the Lord Lasky from his capitaynate in Livonia, and I wrote answer agayn. Jan. 10th, this day death seased on him. This day at none dyed Edward Maynard just on yere old. Jan. 11th, buried this day at ten of the clok. Jan. 15th, Mr. Ashley, the clerk of the cownsayle, his wife and whole family removed from my howse in Mortlak to theyr howse in London in Holborn, with all his whole family. He and she had used me, my wife and childern, wurshipfully and bowntifully for our frendeship shewed unto them for the lone of our howse and lodgings from Allhallow-tyde last. Master Maynard allso his howsehold removed the 15th and 16th day to London, and my stable free delivered. Jan. 20th, I sent my letters for the Lord Lasky to be carryed in a shyp of Dansk called the John of Dansk. Jan. 21st, Sonday, about none Wenefryde Goose her sone born and died, and she did [there]uppon for old melancholik pangs destroy herself. Memorandum, my nurse at Barnes had xvjs. more besides the last 40s. in the begynning of this month. Feb. 14th, Francys Dee, she cam from the nurse at Barnes; the woman very unquiet and unthankfull. Feb. 15th, Her Majestie gratiously accepted of my few lynes of thankfulnes delivered unto her by the Cowntess of Warwik hora secunda a meridie at Hampton Court, two or three dayes before the remove to Somerset Howse. Feb. 21st, I borrowed £10 of Mr. Thomas Digges[ll] for one hole yere. Feb. 22nd, a sharp anger betwene me and the Bishop of Leightyn in the towr, for that he wold not shew his farder interest to Nangle: he sayd that after I had seen his brode seal of commendation, that I had institution and induction to the Nangle. Then I sayd his lordship did fable. He there uppon that so moved that he called me spitefully "coniver." I told him that he did lye in so saying, and that I wold try on the fleysh of him, or by a bastaned gown of him, if he wer not prisoner in the Towr. Inter 12^a et 2^a a meridie my sharp anger with the Bishop of Leightyn in the lieftenante's dyning parlor before the Lieutenant Sir Michael Blunt. Mr. Liewtenat Nant and Mr. Blunt are wittnesses. March

12th and 13th, these two nights I dremed much of Mr. Kelly, as if he wer in my howse familiar with his wife and brother. March 17th, Francis Garland cam home and browght me a letter from Mr. Thomas Kelly. I made acquayntance with Syr Thomas Chaloner, Knight, who married sergeant Fletewood's dowghter; Mr. Thomas Webbes was the meanes. At six after none receyved from Mr. Francis Nicholls £15, part of one hundred pounds, the rest whereof £85 is to be receyved from Mr. Nicolls within a fortnight after the Annunciation of Our Lady next; and after that in the beginning of June £100, and in Julie the third hundred powndes: and I am to teach him the conclusion of fixing and teyning the moon, &c.

ll.   This notice is particularly interesting, showing the intimate connexion which existed between the first English mathematician of the day and the philosopher of Mortlake.

April 3rd, Bartilmew Hikman and Robert Charles cam up. Letice cam with Barthilmew, and went away agayn. April 8th, Letice cam agayn from Barnet to my servyse. I receyved £50 of Mr. Nichols. April 9th, I gave Barthilmew Hikman £12 in new angels to give and pay to Robert Charles, which he had payd for him at Michelmas last. I gave him allso a double pistolet for his courtesy. Little Adolph Webbes cam to me. April 10th, Barthilmew and Robert Charles went homward. May 7th, Thomas Richardson of Bissham cam to Mortlak to me. May 9th, he and Mr. Laward of the Chandry cam. Our court day at Wymbledon. May 11th, mane hora octava William Emery of Danbery in Essex became my retayner at Mortlak, commended by Mr. Thanet of Rushmer by Ypswich, borne 1568, Julii 4. I gave Robert Web 10*s.* Richard 10*s.* and Elizabeth 3*s.* in the begynning of this month. May 21st, be it remembered that on this xxj. day of May I bargayned with and bowght of Mr. Mark Perpoint, of Mortlak, that next mansion howse with the plat, and all the appertenances abowt it for £32, as the sayd Mr. Perpoint of late had at the last court-day bowght it, and had surrender of it unto him made of Thomas Knaresborowgh for £25 to mydsommer next. Abowt two of the clok after none, before Jane my wife in the strete, I gave him a saffron noble in ernest for a drink peny. Mr. Hawkins, of London, at that instant cam to have bowght it. May 27th, Mr. Francys Blunt, brother to the late Lord Mountjoy, unkle to the Lord Mowntjoy living, and to Sir Charles of the court, cam to be acquaynted to me, he having byn a travayle at Constantinople. June 4th, Barthilmew Hikman cam to Mortlak in the morning. June 22nd, I had my copy of Mr. Roger Dale our stuard, and had £5 the fine released of the Lord his bowntifullnes. I told the stuard that I had bowght the howse of Mr. Mark Perpoynt, and he desyred to see the note of his copy, and so I did. I told Mr. Perpoint that I had byn at London to prepare his mony, and I told him that I had seen the court-roll for his copy. I went to London to fetch the £32 for Mr. Perpoint, and so I sent him word. This evening I browght the mony, but he was gon to bed. This morning I tendered the mony, and told it at goodman Welder's before Mr. Stokden, and goodman Welder, but Mr. Perpoint refused to perform the bargayn. Deus bene vertat!

July 13th, I gave to Robert 5s. upon his wagis this day. July 14th, I gave 4s. to Letise, part of her noble for her quarter wagis, ending the 9th day of this month. July 18th, I bowght goodman Welder his hovel, which is in the yard of the howse next me, which I bowght of Mr. Mark Perpoint. I gave him a new angel and five new shillings, and he is to have more 5s., that is 20s. in all; and if I cannot compact to enter the howse, then hee is to tak his hovel, and to restore it to me. July 21st, I give to Richard 5s. uppon his wagis this day. July 22nd, I payd Mr. Childe £7. 13s. 4d. for all his wood, xx. lode and vj. July 24th, the offer for the bargayn agayn of Mr. Perpoynt's behalf: this is Mr. Stokden's doing. July 27th, remember that this Friday I payd Mr. Tomson £4 for his master Mr. Herbert, which I borrowed 12th of December 1592: and Mr. Herbert sent it agayn to my furder use by Mistres Lee. Aug. 7th, Mystres Twyne and Mystres Banister cam to viset me. Mr. Bele and Mrs. Bele, Mistres

Plan, Mrs. Parpoint, &c. dyned with me. I gave Robert Web 5*s.*; he sent it to Mr. Homes. Aug. 9th, I dyned with the Lord Keper at Kew. Aug. 17th, I and my wife and Katharin our dowghter dyned with the Lord Keper at Kew. Aug. 28th, I was all day with the Lord Keper. Mr. Web and the philosopher cam. Aug. 29th, Mr. Web and the philosopher cam again. Aug. 30th, Mistres Redhed, mother to Mr. John Ponsoys by her first husbond, Mr. Gubbens, bokebynder, and his wife, and the same day Mr. Redhed himself, one of her Majestie's jentlemen hushers, cam to me. Sept. 11th, Jana, post triduunam ægrotationem abortiebatur, mane hora decima. Sept. 13th, the howse surrendered for me by Mr. Mark Perpoint, Mr. William Walker of Wimbledon, Miles Holland, Mr. John Stockden, the thre customarie tenants, with promys to bring in his wife at the next court day to surrender. Sept. 18th, Elizabeth Kyrton had *2s. 6d.* Sept. 20th, Barthilmew Hikman cam to Mortlak, and Robert Charles. I gave Robert Web 5*s.* by Arthur. Sept. 26th, Mr. Herbert went toward the court, and so toward Waty. Sept. 28th, tempestuous, windy, clowdy, hayl and rayn, after three of the clok after none. Remember that the last day of this month Elizabeth Kyrton, who had served me twelve yeres, five yeres uppon prentiship and seven for wagis, five yeres therof for four nobles a yere, and the two last for five nobles the yere, was payd her full payment now remayning due: whereuppon she receyved £4. 4*s.* for her due of wagis remayning; and I gave her moreover an half angel new in gold, and my wife another; Arthur half-a-crown for him and his brother; Katharyn half-a-crown for her and her sister. And so she wente from my servyce uppon no due cause known to me.

Oct. 4th, Sir Edward Keley set at liberty by the Emperor. Oct. 12th, Mr. Cornelio Camaiere cam from the Lord Lasky from Livonia. Oct. 15th, Margerie Thornton cam to my servyce. Oct. 18th, before Mr. Perpoint, Miles Holland, Robert Wellder, William Beck surrendred my cottage agayn unto me, and I payd him £5, the full £12 as it cost him. To Letice two shillings. Oct. 20th, Mr. Cornelio went toward the flete of Stade to returne. Oct. 24th, Ostende besieged by report. Not true. Oct. 25th, Mr.

Gray, the Lady Cumberland's preacher, his wrangling and denying and despising alchimicall philosophers. Nov. 5th. Mr. Francys Nicolls, Mr. Prise, Mr. Nores. Nov. 18th, Jane most desperately angry in respect of her maydes. Nov. 20th, Margery went and Dorothe Legg cam for 30*s.* yerely. Margery Thornton was dismissed from my servyce to Mrs. Child, and Dorothe Leg cam by Mrs Mary Revel's sending the same day and howr, hora tertia after none. Nov. 26th, John, sometymes Mr. Colman's servant, cam to me from the Lady Cowntess of Cumberland. Dec. 3rd, the Lord Willowghby his bowntifull promys to me. The Cowntess of Kent, his syster, and the Cowntess of Cumberland visited me in the afternone. The Lord Willowghby dyned with me. Dec. 4th, £20 Lord Willughby. Dec. 5th, the newes of Sir Edward Kelly his libertie. Dec. 11th, I gave Robert 20*s.* at his going to London with my wife. Dec. 22nd, I gave Robert two shillings. Dec. 24th, Mr. Webbes committed to the Marshalsea. Dec. 25th, this night Mr. Webbes got out, and taken this day (the 26th).

1594. Jan. 3rd, the Lord Keper sent my wife 20 angels in a new red velvet purse, cira occasum solis paulo ante. Jan. 4th, D. Michael Peiserus, Doctor Medicus Marchionis Brandeburgensis, me humanissime invisit. Jan. 5th, a very tempestuous wyndy night. Jan. 9th, Robert Thickpeny from Sir Richard Martyn, and Miles Holland, baylif for the Lord of the Manor, sealed up Mr. Webb's chest, and case of boxes. Jan. 19th, the cobler with the mad woman. Jan. 25th, I sent my letters to Mr. Lording for Mr. Pontoys to Dantsiz. Jan. 26th, I cam to Mr. Web to the Marshalsea. Jan. 27th, Thomas Richardson cam while I was at London, and so I fownd him at home; and agayn he promised me his working of forty dayes. Jan. 28th, Mr. Vander Laen promised on 26 day to begyn his work of fixing *lunam*. Madinia somwhat sickly. Robert Wood, visitted with spirituall creatures, had comfort by conference. Jan. 31st, Mr. Vander Laen began his work of *luna*, five myle sowth from Glocester. Mr. Morgan Treherne told me of Mr. Lawrence of eighty yeres old. Mr. Thomas Sharp, chief stuard to the Lady Russell at Bisham, is master and good frende to Thomas Richardson, as he himselfe told me. Theodore Dee from the myddle of this month had his left ey blud-shotten from the side next his temple, very sore bludshotten, above thre wekes contynuing. Feb. 1st, Mr. John Ask sent me two little dubble gilt bowles waying thirteen ownces and a half. Feb. 7th, Sir Thomas Wilks offer philosophicall cam to my hands by Mr. Morice Kiffyn. This day the Archbishop of Canterbury inclined sometyme to the request of dispensation. Feb. 20th, 21st, Theodor fell sick in the Shrovtyde weke, and so into a tertian ague. March 10th, uppon a flight of feare bycause of Mr. Webbes his sending for me to come to him to the Marshalsea, now when he looked to be condemned on the Monday or Tuesday next. March 16th, Barthilmew Hikman cam up. March 18th, Mr. Heriot cam to me. March 20th, I did before Barthilmew Hikman pay Letice her full yere's wagis ending the 7th day of Aprill next; her wagis being four nobles, an apron, a payr of hose and shoes. March 23rd, I gave Barthilmew Hikman the nag which the Lord Keper had given me. Barthilmew Hikman and William his brother went homward. Magus disclosed by frendeship of Mr. Richard Alred. A συδδεν πανγ οφ ανγερ βετυυενε Μ. Νικολς ανδ με. March 28th, Mr. Francis Garland browght me Sir Edward Kelley and his brother's letters. March 31st, a great fit of the stone in my left kydney: all day I could do but three or four drops of water, but I drunk a draught of white wyne and salet oyle, and after that, crabs' eys in powder with the bone in the carp's head, and abowt four of the clok I did eat tosted cake buttered, and with suger and nutmeg on it, and drunk two great draughts of ale with it; and I voyded within an howr much water, and a stone as big as an Alexander seed. God be thanked! Five shillings to Robert Webb, part of his wagis.

April 1st, Capitayn Hendor made acquayntance with me, and shewed me a part of his pollicy against the Spanishe King his intended mischief agaynst her Majestie and this realme. April 4th, John Stokden cam to study with our children. Mr. Thomas Wye cam with a token from Mistres Ashley. Remove to Mr. Harding and Mr. Abbot at Oxford abowt my Arabik boke. April 5th, my right ey very sore and bludshotten. April 7th, Mr. Nicols cam agayn out of Northampton. Mr. Barret and Mistres

Barret cam to visit me. May 3rd, betwene 6 and 7 after none the Quene sent for me to her in the privy garden at Grenwich, when I delivered in writing the hevenly admonition, and Her Majestie tok it thankfully. Onely the Lady Warwyk and Sir Robert Cecill his Lady wer in the garden with Her Majestie. May 18th, Her Majestie sent me agayn the copy of the letter of G. K. with thanks by the Lady Warwick. May 21st, Sir John Wolley moved my sute to Her Majesty. She graunted after a sort, but referred all to the Lord of Canterbury. May 25th, Dr. Awbrey moved my sute to Her Majesty, and answere as before. May 29th, with the Archbishop before the Quene cam to her house. June 3rd, I, my wife, and seven children, before the Quene at Thisellworth. My wife kissed her hand. I exhibited my request for the Archbishop to com to my cottage. June 6th, supped with the Lord Archbishop. Invited him to my cottage. June 11th, given to Robert Webb at London seven shillings in the begynning of this month. June 15th, £40 of Mr. Thomas Harward. I shuld have £60 more. A great fytt of the stone in my kydneys. June 20th, Mistres Magdalen Perpoynt was sole examined of our Stuard at the Temple. June 22nd, morgaged my late purchas to Mr. Richard White for £30, to be received within a few dayes. June 23rd, I discharged Robert Web of my service, and gave him 40 shillings for a full satisfaction of all things. Thomas Richardson cam and offered me his work and labor, and had, as he requested, my letter to Mr. Thomas Sharpe. June 24th, on Midsommer Day Antony Ryve Taylor cam to my service, for wagis by the yere three pounds and a livery. Barthilmew Hikman cam. June 26th, I discharged Jane Hikman to go with her father Barthilmew home into Northamptonshire, and gave her ten shillings, and promised her at Hallowtyd ten shillings more. Barthilmew Hikman and Goodman Ball with Jane Hikman went homward. June 29th, after I had hard the Archbishop his answers and discourses, and that after he had byn the last Sonday at Tybald's with the Quene and Lord Threasorer, I take myself confounded for all suing or hoping for anything that was. And so adiew to the court and courting tyll God direct me otherwise!

The Archbishop gave me a payre of sufferings to drinke. God be my help as he is my refuge! Amen.

July 1st, I gave Robert yet more a French crown for a farwell. July 2nd, given to Richard ten shillings uppon his wagis. July 6th, Michael becam distempered in his hed and bak. July 9th, in the morning began my hed to ake and be hevy more then of late, and had some wambling in my stomach. I had broken my fast with sugar sopps, &c. I gave Letice my servant 5*s*. part of her wagis: with part whereof she was to buy a smok and neckercher. July 13th, in ortu solis Michael Dee did give up the ghost after he sayd, "O Lord, have mercy uppon me!" July 19th, goodman Richardson began his work. Aug. 19th, Elizabeth Felde cam to my servyce: she is to have five nobles the yere and a smok. Aug. 26th, Mr. Gherardt, the chirurgion and herbalist, [cam to me]. Aug. 30th, Monsieur Walter Mallet toke his leave of me to go home to Tholose. He had the fix oyle of saltpetre. Sept. 18th, I sent letters to Sir Ed. K. and T. Kelly, between 10 and 2 after none taken from the dore.

Oct. 3rd, I payd Mrs. Stockden £4 I borrowed of her; I payd her 26*s*. 8*d*. for four loade of wood. I remayn debter for a load of hay, and for 400 of billet in forks. Oct. 4th, payd Mr. Childe £3. 10*s*. for ten lode of lose faggot. Oct. 14th, Mr. Robert Thomas cam to my howse to dwell. Oct. 28th, hora 6½ a meridie, I writ and sent a letter to the Lady Skydmor, in my wife's name, to move her Majestie that eyther I might declare my case to the body of the cownsayle, or else under the great seale to have lycens to go freely anywhither. Oct. 31st, lightening without thunder in the afternone and in the night following.

Nov. 24th, receyved a letter from Sir Edward Kelley by Rowley. Dec. 2nd, Francys Garland cam to England from Prage. Just five yeres past I cam to England from Breame as Francis Garland cam now: but the Stade flete stayed at Harwich. The 2nd of our cold December, Barthilmew was preferred by me to the Lord Willoughby his servyce at Barbican, in the presence of the Cowntess of Kent: and the Lord Willoughby did presently write his warrant to Mr. Jonson in Fletestreet, taylor, to deliver to Barthilmew his cloth and couishins, and so it was to Barthilmew delivered immediately. Dec. 7th, Jane my wife delivered her supplication to the Quene's Majestie, as she passed out of the privy garden at Somerset Howse to go to diner to the Savoy to Syr Thomas Henedge. The Lord Admirall toke it of the Quene. Her Majestie toke the bill agayn and kept it uppon her cushen; and on the 8th day, by the chief motion of the Lord Admirall, and somwhat of the Lord Buckhurst, the Quene's wish was to the Lord Archbishop presently that I shuld have Dr. Day his place in Powles. Dec. 22nd, payd seven shillings to Elizabeth Felde, part of her wagis. Given to Lettyce *5s.*, part of her wagis. Payd to Richard *8s.*, part of his wagis; and all other reckonings payd.

1595. Jan. 8rd, the Wardenship of Manchester spoken of by the Lord Archbishop of Canterbury. Feb. 5th, my bill of Manchester offered to the Quene afore dynner by Sir John Wolly to signe, but she deferred it. Feb. 10th, at two after none I toke a cutpurse taking my purse out of my pocket in the Temple. Feb. 18th, Mr. Laward his sonne Thomas born at noone or a little after, ¼ vel ½. Consultatio et deliberatio prima cum Marmione Haselwood in fine istius mensis. March 18th, Mr. Francis Garland cam this morning to viset me, and had much talk with me of Sir E. K. March 20th, Mr. Marmion Haselwood, Mr. Dymmock, and Mr. Hipwell, cam to me to Mortlak. March 21st, Barthilmew Hikman cam to Mortlak. March 26th, Barthilmew homeward. March 29th, Mr. Laward and Mr. Alred cam to me.

April 18th, my bill for Manchester Wardenship signed by the Quene, Mr. Herbert offring it her. May 4th, payd Richard *20s.* part of his wagis, and more I gave him *10s.* for full payment of all od reckenings of late. May 5th, Mr. Cave dyed. May 8th, the Master of the Rolls his curtesy, thowgh I had never spoken unto him. May 9th, my coosen John Awbry cam to me, to recreate himselfe for a while. May 21st, I discharged Letice of my servyce, and payd all duetyes untyll this day, her yere ending on the 8th of Aprill. I gave her for a month over *2s. 6d.* and for to spend by the way I gave her *2s. 6d.*, Robert Charles and my wife being by in my study. May 25th, 26th, 27th, the Signet, the Privy Seale, and the Great Seale of the Wardenship; £3. 12*s.* borrowed of my brother Arnold. June 1st, my yong coosen, John Awbrey, was sent for to his father to London. Mr. Partrich, his brother, in London; Richard Ward, and other cam for him. June 9th, Barthilmew Hikman went homeward. June 11th, I wrote to the Erle of Derby, his secretary, abowt Manchester. June 18th, Anne Powell cam to my service; she is to have four nobles by the yere, a payr of hose and shoes. June 21st, the Erle of Derby his letter to Mr. Warren for the colledge. June 25th, Dr. Awbrey died at midnight. My cosen, Mr. George Broke, gave me £50 in gold, hora tertia a meridie. June 29th, Mr. John Blayney, of Over Kingesham in Radnorshyre, and Mr. Richard Baldwyn, of Duddlebury in Shropshyre, visited me at Mortlak. The great-grandfather of the sayd John, and my great-grandmother by the father side, were brother and sister.

July 1st, the two brethren, Master Willemots, of Oxfordshire, cam to talk of my howse hyring. Master Baynton cam with Mistres Katharyn Hazelwood, wife to Mr. Fuller. July 7th, Mr. Morgan Jones, my cosen, cam to me at Mistres Walls twise. July 12th, Mr. Goodier, of Manchester, cam to me. Dies natalis. July 15th, I gave Mr. Morgan Traharn his bill to Mr. Harbert. July 25th, Mrs. Mary Nevell cam. July 28th, a letter from Mr. Oliver Carter, Fellow of Manchester College. I writt agayn to him the same day. July 29th, Mistres Mary Nevel went to London, and so into Kent. July 31st, the Cowntess of Warwik did this evening thank her Majestie in my name, and for me, for her gift of the Wardenship of Manchester. She toke it gratiously; and was sorry that it was so far from hens, but that some better thing neer hand shall be fownd for me; and, if opportunitie of tyme wold serve, her Majestie wold speak with me herself. I had a bill made by Mr. Wood, one of the clerks of the signet, for the first frutes given me by her Majestie. Aug. 2nd, at Mr. Cosener his table at Grenewich: I spak that wich greatly liked Mr. Sergeant Oliver Lloyd; wold have disputed agayn. Aug. 5th, very rayny all day, and had the wynde north E. and W. Aug. 12th, I receyved Sir Edward Kellyes letters of the Emperor's, inviting me to his servyce again. Aug. 14th, peperit Jana (nutu Dei) circa horam quartam a meridie. Aug. 27th, Margarite Dee baptized hora 4½ a meridie. Godfather, the Lord Keper; his deputy, Mr. Crowne. Godmothers, the Cowntess of Cumberland, her deputy Mistres Davis; and the Cowntess of Essex, her deputy Mistres Bele. Barthilmew Hikman cam to Mortlak on his own busines. Sept. 2nd, the spider at ten of the clok at night suddenly on my desk, and suddenly gon; a most rare one in bygnes and length of feet. I was in a great study at my desk. Sept. 6th I gave Richard 2s. 6d. part of his wagis, when he went to his grandfather. Sept. 13th, I dyned with the Erle of Derby at Russell Howse, Mr. Thymothew and Mr. John Statfeldt, German, being there. Sept. 14th, to Elizabeth Feeld 2s. for the taylor. Sept. 22nd, Elizabeth Feeld went from my servyce. I dined with the Erle of Darby. Sept. 26th, £6 borrowed of my cosen William Hetherley for fourteen days to pay for Barthilmew Hikman. Sept. 29th, Margery Stubble of Hownslow, our dry nurse, entred into the yere of her servyce begynning on Michaelmas Day, and is to have £3 her yeres wagis and a gown cloth of russet. Edward Edwards began his yere of serving me allso on Michelmas Day, and he must have 40s. for his yere's wagis, and a lyvery.

Oct. 7th, my anger (hor. 5 a mer.) with Edward my coke, bycause of his disorder. Oct. 8th, Mr. Richard Western lent me £10 for a yere. Oct. 9th, I dyned with Syr Walter Rawlegh at Durham Howse. Oct. 11th, to Edward 2s., part of wagis. Mr. Banks lent me uppon lone tyll after Christmas £5. Mr. Emery sent me £3 by my servant Richard Walkedine. Oct. 14th, to Anne 2s. part of wagis; to Elizabeth Felde payd the rest of her yeres wagis, and moreover 2s. 6d. given for the overplus tyme. Oct. 19th, the old reckoning betwene me and Edmond Hilton made clere. Of his eleven pownds demanded, I shewd him of my old note that he had receyved £6. 15s., and after that Sted his 25s., and Mr. Emery his £3 lent him; as I did shew him Sted his letter, and Mr. Emery his letter of the last month. All these sommes make just an eleven pownd. Payd to nurse Stubble, in part of payment of her wagis, 5s. Oct. 20th, to Anne 12d. Richard rode toward Oxford for my Arabik boke. Oct. 25th, Sted was a suter to me for help in law against his father. Nov. 8th, my goods sent me by Peravall toward Manchester. Nov. 19th, my Arabik boke restored by God's favor. Nov. 21st, goodwife Lidgatt payd her rent two quarters ending at the feast of the Annunciation of our Lady next, 13s. 4d. Goodman Agar was by in my hall at Mortlak. Nov. 25th, the newes that Sir Edward Kelley was slayne. Nov. 26th, Mr. Nicolas Bagwell of Manchester browght me a letter from my brother Arnold. Lent to Mister Laurence Dutton twelve shillings. My wife and children all by water toward Coventry. Dec. 10th, Mr. Lok his Arabik bokes and letter to me by Mr. Berran his sonne. Dec. 23rd, I payd to John Norton, stationer, ten pownds in hand, and was bownd in a recognisance before Doctor Hone for the payment of the rest, £10 yerely, at Christmas and Midsommer £5, tyll £53 more 14s. 8d. were payd. Receyved £30 in part of payment of one hundred for my howse at Manchester of Mr. Paget. Dec. 26th, nata filia Comitis Derby mane circa quartam horam Londini.

1596. Feb. 15th, I cam to Manchester a meridie hora quinta. Feb. 20th, enstalled in Manchester wardenship inter nonam et undecimam horam ante meridiem. March 14th, warning given publikely against Thomas Goodyer. March 21st, warning given publikly of licence given to Thomas Goodyer.

April 2nd, Sir John Byron, knight, and Mr. John Byron, esquier, dyned with me in the colledg. I moved the matter of Xyd an aker of hay grownd of his tenants. He promised well. April 6th, I went to Mr. Ashton of Lester and to Mr. Sherington. April 8th, Margaret Dee begonne to be weaned. May 7th, possession taking in Salford. May 11th, my brother Aubrey and Richard toward London. June 3rd, I gave Antony Cowly 20s. and discharged him. June 4th, Antony Cowley went yerely from my howse, I know not whither. June 14th, Mr. Harry Savill, the antiquary, cam to me. June 15th, I wrote by Mr. Harry Savill of the book dwelling at Hallyfax to Christopher Saxton at Denningley. I sent my letter to Sir Robert Cecill's howse by William Debdell. June 18th, the commission for the colledge sent to London to be engrossed in the Duchy office. I sent by Nicholas Baguely of Newton to Mr. Brogreton and to William Nicolson to follow it this terme. June 21st, Mr. Christopher Saxton cam to me. June 22nd, entred upon great Brereridings in Salford. June 24th, Barthilmew cam. June 25th, order taken by the sherif betwene me and Raf Holden. June 26th, the Erle of Derby with the Lady Gerard, Sir . . . Molyneux and his Lady, dawghter to the Lady Gerard, Master Hawghton and others, cam suddenly uppon ^{mc} after three of the clok. I made them a skoler's collation, and it was taken in good part. I browght his honor and the ladyes to Ardwyk Grene toward Lyme, at Mr. Legh his howse, twelve myles of. June 29th, wyndy and rayny. July 5th, Mr. Savill and Mr. Saxton cam. July 6th, I, Mr. Saxton and Arthur Rouland, John and Richard, to Howgh Hall. July 9th, I sent Roger Kay of Manchester with my letters into Wales. July 10th, Manchester town described and measured by Mr. Christopher Saxton. Given to nurse Stubley 10s., part of wagis. July 10th to 14th, occupied with low controversies, as with Holden of Salford and the tenants of Sir John Byron of Faylsworth in the right of the colledge, sending to . . . to the cownty, and sending for Mr. Tyldesley or Chester for cownsaylers. July 12th, given more to nurse, when her sonne John Stubley went from me toward London to be reconcyled to his master. I gave him 5s. The yong man, Leon the hatter, went with him. July 14th, Mr. Saxton rode away. The sessions day at Manchester. July 19th, Ales cam by Mrs. Beston's help to my servyce. Thomas, my coke, went from me. July 21st, Isabell Bardman from the chamber to the kitchin. July 25th, thunder in the morning; rayne in the night. July 27th, the Erle of Darby went by London ward; dyned at Curtes' howse. Aug. 10th, Mr. Thomas Jones of Tregarron cam to me to Manchester and rode toward Wales bak agayn the 13th day to mete the catall coming. Aug. 13th, I rid toward York. Halifax and Mr. Thomas Jones rode toward Wales. Aug. 20th, I cam to Manchester from York. Aug. 20th to 27th, much disquietnes and controversy abowt the tythe corne of Hulme. Aug. 30th, Cromsall corne-tyth obteyned by consent, but afterwards dowted and half denyed; then utterly denyed. Sept. 1st, Mary Goodwyn cam to my servyce to govern and teach Madinia and Margaret, my yong dowghters. Sept. 3rd, being Fryday, I rode to Syr John Byron's, to Royton, to talk with him abowt the controversy betwene the colledg and his tenants. He pretented that we have part of Faylesworth Common within our Newton Heath, which cannot be proved I am sure. We wer agreed that James Traves (being his bayly) and Francis Nutthall, his servant for him, shold with me understand all circumstances, and so duely to procede. Sept. 5th, seventeen hed of cattell from my kinsfolk in Wales by the curteous Griffith David, nephew to Mr. Thomas Griffith, browght.

Oct. 26th, Mr. Francis Nicols and Barthilmew cam to Manchester. Oct. 29th, they rode homeward. Nov. 22nd, £4. 6s. given to my wife by Mr. Francys Wodcote. Dec. 3rd, Mr. Palmer cam to be curate.

1597. Jan. 19th, I sent £4 to Barthilmew Hikman by Bradshaw the carryer. Jan. 22nd, Olyver Carter's thret to sue me with proces from London was this Satterday in the church declared to the clerk. Feb. 5th, Rich. Key of Weram cwrate cam to me by Mr. Heton's information, and I to try him three monthes for 50s. wagis. Feb. 7th, John Morryce came to Manchester. Feb. 11th, £5 borowed of Mr. Mat. Heton. Feb. 14th, this Monday John Morrise went with my letters to Mr. John Gwyn, and twelve more in Montgomeryshyre, esquyers. Feb. 17th, delivered to Charles Legh the elder my silver tankard with the cover, all dubble gilt, of the Cowntess of Herford's gift to Francis her goddoughter, waying 22 oz. great waight, to lay in pawn in his owne name to Robert Welsham the goldsmith for £4 tyll within two dayes after May-day next. My dowghter Katharin and John Crocker and I myself (John Dee) were at the delivery of it and waying of it in my chamber: it was wrapped in a new handkercher cloth. Feb. 25th, Mr. Heton borrowed the Concordantiæ Majores Roberti Stephani. He hath allso my boke *De Coena* of Doctor Pezelia. March 7th, Mr. Heton lent me £5 more, and thereuppon I gave him a bill of my hand for the whole ten pownd, to be payd at Michelmas next. The other £5 was receyved the 11th of February last. March 17th, Barthilmew Hikman cam. March 19th, I lent Mr. Hopwood *Wierus de præstigiis Dæmonum*.

April 10th, a supplication exhibited by the parishioners. April 11th, 12th, trubblesom days abowt Mr. Palmer the curate. April 15th, I had my *Wierus de præstigiis Dæmonum* from Mr. Hopwood, and lent him *Flagellum Dæmonum* and *Fustio Dæmonum* in 8vo, for tyme till Midsomer. April 21st, I sent Barthilmew Hikman 40*s*. I sent by Bradshaw many letters to London. I sent by goodman Thurp of Salford my great letter to the byshop of Lincolne, and one to Mr. Shallcross. April 22nd, after none Sir Urien Legh knight, and his brother, and Mr. Brown, and Mr. George Booth, sherif of Chesshire, did viset me. Mr. Booth sayd that he wold yeld that to me that he wold not yeld to the bisshop nor any other. Mr. Wortley of Wortley cam allso the same day hora quarta a meridie. May 2nd, Mr. Hulme and Mr. Williamson cam to me in the Lord Bishop of Lincoln's case for Hulme. May 4th, I, with Sir Robert Barber, curat, and Robert Talsley, clerk of Manchester parish church, with diverse of the town of divers ages, went in perambulation to the bownds of Manchester parish: began at the Leeless Bench against Prestwich parish, and so had a vew of the thre corne staks, and then down tyll Mr. Standysh new enclosure on the Low, wher we stayed and vewed the stak yet standing in the bank of the dich, being from the corne a eleven measures of Mr. Standley's stak then in his hand, and two fote more, which still I did measure afterward, and it did conteyn in Kentish feete 6 ynches and thre quarters. The survey geometricall of the very circuits of Manchester parish was ended in this, being the sixth day of my work. May 11th, the way to Stopford surveyed by John Cholmeley and John Crocker. May 17th, to Richard Walkeden 20*s*. of his wagis payd. May 20th, the Lady Booth made acquayntance here. May 23rd, to Isabell Boordman 8*s*. 8*d*. to make up whole yere's wagis due at the Annunciation of our Lady last past. I allowed to Mr. Williamson ten dayes respite more for his kinsman to bring in his evidence for the process of the proceedings. Payd to nurse 3*s*. to make up her full payment of her yere's wagis ended at Michaelmas last. May 27th, open enmitie with Palmer before Sir Edward Fitton. Sir Edward Fitton told Matthew Palmer to his face that he had known him to be a mutinous man and a . . . June 9th, Thomas Sankinson told me of John Basset his coming to London. June 14th, the unlawfull assembly and rowte of William Cutcheth, Captayn Bradley, John Taylor, Rafe Taylor, at Newton, against my men, describing the rumour of Newton. June 27th, newes from Hull of 23 barrells of Dansk rye sent me from John Pontoys.

July 1st, I sent Roger Kay to Vanydles for catall. July 4th, the carriers to Wakefeld for the corn. July 5th, toward evening lightning and little thunder. July 6th, thunder in the morning. July 7th, five horse lode of Dansk ry cam home. July 19th, the strang pang of my back opening mane hora 6¼. In the church uppon Mr. Palmer's disorder against Mr. Lawrence. July 20th, the last of my Dansk rye, in all 21 horse load. Aug. 6th, this night I had the vision and shew of many bokes in my dreame, and among the rest was one great volume thik in large quarto, new printed, on the first page whereof as a title in great letters was printed "Notus in Judæa Deus." Many other bokes methowght I saw new printed, of very strange arguments. I lent Mr. Edward Hopwood of Hopwood my *Malleus Maleficarum* to use tyll new yere's tyde next, a short thik old boke with two clasps, printed anno 1517. Aug. 19th, the Erle and Cowntess of Derby cam to Alport lodg. Aug. 21st, the Erle and Cowntess of Derby had a banket at my lodging at the colledge hora 4½. Aug. 27th, John Addenstall from Mr. Emery. I wrote. Sept. 3rd, Mr. Werall of Lobester within two miles of Donkaster cam to me to be acquaynted with me. Sept. 9th, very wyndy at Sowth and rayny. Sept. 12th, hayle this morning on Monday. Sept. 15th, lent by Mr. Werall 40*s*. John Cholmley went with him to give him and other physik; and I answered John Cholmeley the 40*s*. again. Sept 24th, Barthilmew cam. Sept. 25th, Mr. Olyver Carter his impudent and evident disolutenes in the church. Sept. 26th, he repented and some pacification was made. Sept. 27th, I granted a lease of thre lives to Mr. Ratclyf for two howses in Dene Square of 7*s*. rent both;

fine, twenty nobles. Sept. 28th, cam Mr. Yardely of Calcot in Chesshyre, abowt six myles wide of Chester, toward the Holt. Nova de philosopho D. Waldero. Sept. 30th, John Crockar (my good servant) had leave to go to see his parents. He went with Barthilmew Hikman and Robert Charles toward Branbroke, with Arthur Golding, to cure of his fistula. John Crocker intendeth to returne abowt Easter or at Whitsuntyde next. God be his spede! Mr. Humphry Damport made our stuard.

Oct. 12th, Rafe Holden preferred a bill against Richard Walkeson for Brereriding's chase entyring, which I and Antony Ryve . . . fals. The bill was not fownd. Oct. 22nd, John Fletcher of Manchester went with my letters to Vanylos this Sunday morning. Nov. 3rd, Mr. John Cholmeley toward London by Market-Harborow. Nov. 7th, the fellows and the receyver agreed not with me in accounts. Paulo post nonam mane Arthur's left eye hurt at playing at fence with rapier and dagger of sticks, by a foyne of Edmond Arnold. Nov. 10th, Mr. Burch his letter from Mathew Palmer. Nov. 14th, the fellows wold not graunt me the £5. for my howse-rent, as the Archbishops had graunted: and our foundation commaundeth an howse. Nov. 17th, I sent Ed. Arnold to London on fote with my letters to D. Julio. Dec. 3rd, to Richard Walkeden 10s. in part of wagis. To nurse 10s. Dec. 9th, I visited the grammar schole. Dec. 13th, I wrote by the carryer Barret to D. Cæsar. Dec. 14th, Mr. George Broke, sonne to Mr . . . Broke of . . ., cam to be acquaynted with me, whome I used most frendely. Mr. Ratclif of Manchester cam with him, but Mr. Heton allso cam on Tuesday after none when I had no leyser. Dec. 17, I lent to Mr. Barlow for his sonne a Spanish grammer in 8vo. printed at Lovayn in anno 1555 by Bartholomæus Gravay in Spanish, French, and Latin. To R. Dickonson I payd £7. 2s. for the plate and a new bell made till 1599, January 1st, £66.

1598. Jan. 4th, I wrote to Barthilmew and Charles by Bradshaw. Jan. 17th, my brother Arnold to Chester and Vaunlos. Jan. 18th, Ed. Arnold with my letter to London. Jan. 19th, hora secunda a meridie I cam before the justices against James Shallcross and John Lawrence for misusing my name to deceyve Mr. Harrughby. Jan. 20th, Walter Fletcher, chirurgien, from Barthilmew Hikman cam. Jan. 22nd, after midnight the college gate toward Hunt's Hall did fall, and som parte of the wall going down the lane. I receyved letters from Mr. John Pontoys. Jan. 24th, Walter Fletcher went with my letters to Barthilmew Hikman and Robert Charles. Amaritudo mea circa mediam noctem. Jan. 28th, the cloose was hyerd of Ed. Brydock for thre pownd payd beforehand by me John Dee to the said Ed. Brydock, being £4 from Candlemas next tyll Candlemas come a twelvemonth. Feb. 9th, George Birch sute was stayd at Chester uppon his promise to compownd with me for all tyth, haye, and other matter. Thomas Goodyer his sute and excommunication I stayed, salvo interim jure suo. Baxter's likewise I stayd at Chester court. Feb. 12th, newes from Mr. Smyth, of Upton personage, cam this Sunday. Feb. 13th, Edmond Arnold to London; thereuppon I sent spedily. Feb. 20th, I wrote by Oliver Ellet, the taylor, to Mr. Nicolls to Faxton. Feb. 22nd, Mr. Nicolls cam and wished to mete Ellet. Feb. 25th, the eclips. A clowdy day, but great darknes abowt 9½ mane. Feb. 26th, circa mediam noctem amaritudo mea. Feb. 27th, Mr. Nicolls rode homeward, and met the messager a little beyond Stopford. I lent Mr. Nicolls home with him Roger Edward's boke to be browght to me by Barthilmew Hikman. March 1st, I receyved Mr. Thynne his letter for Sted's det, and Ed. Arnold his letter of the sute from Upton, and of the Lord Archebisshop his hard dealing. March 2nd, I sent the statute staple to London to Mr. George Brok for Sted. I wrote letters by John Hardy, and sent them in a box. March 5th, newes of Mistres Mary Nevell's death by William Nicholson, that she dyed the Fryday after Candelmas Day. March 11th, borrowed 40*s.* of Mr. George Kenion, of Kersall, to repay againe as sone as I can conveniently. Receyved by Richard Walkeden.

    1600. June 10th, set out from London. Jun. 18th, I, my wife, Arthur Rowland, Mistres Marie Nicols, and Mr. Richard Arnold cam to Manchester.

July 3rd, the Commission set uppon in the Chapter Howse. July 7th, this morning, as I lay in my bed, it cam into my fantasy to write a boke, "De differentiis quibusdam corporum et spirituum." July 8th, I writ to the Lord Bishop of Chester by Mr. Withenstalls. July 10th, Mr. Nicols and Barthilmew Hickman cam. July 14th, Francys Nicols and Barthilmew Hikman went homeward. July 17th, I willed the fellows to com to me by nine the next day. July 18th, it is to be noted of the great pacifications unexpected of man which happened this Friday; for in the forenone (betwene nine and ten) where the fellows were greatly in doubt of my heavy displeasure, by reason of their manifold misusing of themselves against me, I did with all lenity interteyn them, and shewed the most part of the things that I had browght to pass at London for the college good, and told Mr. Carter (going away) that I must speak with him alone. Robert Leigh and Charles Legh were by. Secondly, the great sute betwene Redishmer and me was stayed and by Mr. Richard Holland his wisdom. Thirdly, the organs uppon condition was admitted. And fourthly, Mr. Williamson's resignation granted for a preacher to be gotten from Cambridge. July 19th, I lent Randall Kemp my second part of Hollinshed's Great Chronicle for ij. or iij. wekes. To Newton he restored it. July 31st, we held our audit, I and the fellows for the two yeres last past in my absence, Olyver Carter, Thomas Williamson, and Robert Birch, Charles Legh the elder being receyver. I red and gave unto Mistres Mary Nicolls her prayer.

Aug. 5th, I visited the grammar schole, and fownd great imperfection in all and every of the scholers to my great grief. Aug. 6th, I had a dream after midnight of my working of the philosopher's stone with other. My dreame was after midnight toward day. Aug. 10th, Eucharistam suscepimus, ego, uxor, filia Katharina, et Maria Nicolls. Aug. 30th, a great tempest of mighty wynde S.W. from 2 tyll 6, with rayne.

Sept. 11th, Mr. Holland of Denby, Mr. Gerard of Stopford, Mr. Langley, commissioners from the bishop of Chester, authorized by the bishop of Chester, did call me before them in the church abowt thre of the clok after none, and did deliver to me certayn petitions put up by the fellows against me to answer before the 18th of this month. I answered them all eodem tempore, and yet they gave me leave to write at leiser. Sept. 16th, Mr. Harmer and Mr. Davis, gentlemen of Flyntshire, within four or five myle of Hurden Castell, did viset me. Sept. 29th, I burned before Mr. Nicols, his brother, and Mr. Wortley, all Bartholomew Hikman his untrue actions.mm Sept. 30th, after the departing of Mr. Francis Nicolls, his dowghter Mistres Mary, his brother Mr. William, Mr. Wortley, at my returne from Deansgate, to the ende whereof I browght them on fote, Mr. Roger Kooke offred and promised his faithfull and diligent care and help, to the best of his skill and powre, in the processes chymicall, and that he will rather do so then to be with any in England; which his promise the Lord blesse and confirm! He told me that Mr. Anthony considered him very liberally and frendely, but he told him that he had promised me. Then he liked in him the fidelity of regarding such his promise.

mm. In a note by Dee in MS. Ashm. 488, he says, "All Barthilmew's reports of sight and hering spirituall wer burnt; a copy of the first part, which was afterward fownd, was burnt before me and my wife."

Oct. 13th, be it remembered that Sir Georg Both cam to Manchester to viset Mr. Humfrey Damport, cownsaylor of Gray's Inne, and so cam to the colledg to me; and after a few words of discowrse, we agreed as concerning two or three tenements in Durham Massy in his occupying. That he and I with the fellows wold stand to the arbitrement of the sayd Mr. Damport, after his next return hither from London. John Radclyf, Mr. Damport's man, was with him here, and Mr. Dumbell, but they hard not our agrement; we were in my dyning-room. Oct. 22nd, receyved a kinde letter from the Lord Bishop of Chester in the behalfe of Thomas Billings for a curatship. Nov. 1st, Mr. Roger Coke did begyn to destill. Nov. 4th, the commission and jury did finde the titles of Nuthurst due to Manchester against Mr. James Ashton of Chaterdon. Nov. 7th, Oliver

Carter his . . . before Mr. Birch, Richard Legh and Charles Legh, in the colledg howse. Dec. 2nd, colledg awdit. Allowed my due of £7 yerely for my howse-rent tyll Michelmas last. Arthur Dee a graunt of the chapter clerkship from Owen Hodges, to be had yf £6 wer payd to him for his patent. Dec. 20th, borowed of Mr. Edmund Chetam the scholemaster £10 for one yere uppon plate, two bowles, two cupps with handles, all silver, waying all 32 oz. Item, two potts with cover and handells, double gilt within and without, waying 16 oz.

1601. Jan. 19th, borrowed of Adam Holland of Newton £5 till Hilary day, uppon a silver salt dubble gilt with a cover, waying 14 oz. Feb. 2nd, Roger Cook his supposed plat laying to my discredit was by Arthur my sone fownd by chaunce in a box of his papers in his own handwriting circa meridiem, and after none abowt 1½ browght to my knowledg face to face. O Deus, libera nos a malo! All was mistaken, and we reconcyled godly. Feb. 10th to 15th, reconciliation betwene us, and I did declare to my wife, Katharine my dowghter, Arthur and Rowland, how things wer thus taken. Feb. 18th, Jane cam to my servyce from Cletheraw. Feb. 25th, R. K[oke] pactum sacrum hora octava mane. March 2nd, Mr. Roger Coke went toward London. March 19th, I receyved the long letters from Bartholomew Hickman hora secunda a meridie by a carryer of Oldham. April 6th, Mr. Holcroft of Vale Royall his first acquaintance at Manchester by reason of William Herbert his frend. He used me and reported of me very freely and wurshiply.

CATALOGUS

Librorum Bibliothecæ Externæ
Mortlacensis
D. JOH. DEE, A{o} 1583, 6 SEPT.
LIBRI MANUSCRIPTI.

[From MS. Trin. Coll. Cantab. O. iv. 20, transcribed by Ashmole in MS. Ashm. 1142. Another autograph copy is preserved in MS. Harl. 1879, which scarcely differs from that in the library of Trinity College. The numbers prefixed to the several volumes are added, for the sake of reference, by the Editor.]

1. Milei sphæricorum tractatus tres.

    4° pergameno.

2. Theoricæ planetarum.—Jordani de triangulis, ubi de quadratura circuli.—Ejusdem de perspectiva.—Ejusdem de speculis, crepusculis, ponderibus, speculis comburentibus, lib. ii.

    4° scripti pergameno.

3. Compendium de vitis philosophorum anonymi.—Ursonis de commixtionibus elementorum.—Ejusdem aphorismi.

    4° pergameno.

4. Avicenna de anima mundi, cum aliis, videlicet, Liber cujus initium est, "Inspector præcedentis libri Avicennæ."—Expositorius Rogeri Bachonis.—Liber de ponderibus.—Morienus ad regem Calid.—Rasis libri quinque de deceno (?)—Hermetis libri septem.—Rosinus ad Euthesiam.—Dicta sapientis.—Turba philosophorum.—Distinctionum sapientium liber.—Epistola Alexandri regis Persarum.—Aristoteles de 30 verbis.—Socratis liber.—Effrey Effinensis liber.—Liber Calid.—Liber commentatus.—Opus philosophorum.—Geber de perfecto magisterio.

4° pergameno.

5. Joh. Duns Scoti quæstiones in Porphyrii quinque voces.—Antonii cujusdam expositio in categorias sex, &c.—Rogerii Bachonis de multiplicatione specierum.—Ejusdem perspectiva.

4° pergameno.

6. Thomæ Aquinatis quæstionum disputatarum volumen.

4° pergameno.

7. Scintillarium poetarum.—Summa chiromantiæ.—Ovidii metamorphoseos expositio.—Tractatus de veneno.—Valerius ad Ruffinum de non ducenda uxore, cum expositione.—Joh. Wyclyf determinatio.—Literæ fratris Wilhelmi Fleth.—Fulgentii mythologiæ cum Expositione.—Tractatus de difficilibus dictionibus Bibliæ.—Rob. Lincolniensis in oculo morali.—Rob. Lincolniensis de ratione veneni.—Joh. Walensis breviloquium philosophorum, descriptum per Stoctonem Cantabrigiæ, 1375.—Casus abstracti in jure, per Fratrem Hermannum de provincia Saxoniæ.—Casus episcopo reservati.—Expositio salutationis angelicæ.[1]

4° pergameno.

---

1. Now in Trinity College, Dublin. Bern. 148, (H. 12.)

8.   De ponderibus et mensuris medicinalis operationis.—Viaticus Constantini Africani libri 7.—De modo medendi experimenta.—De origine morborum, et eorum cognitione per urinam.—De electuariis, &c.

4° pergameno.

9.   Ethici Histri cosmographia, ex versione Latina D. Hieronymi.[2]

4° pergameno.

One I had with me, and one I left here, which is noted after.

2.   Now MS. Cotton. Vespas. B. x. thus inscribed by Dr. Dee's hand, "Johannes Dee, 1565, Februarii 21, Wigorniæ, ex dono decani ecclesiæ, Magistri Beddar."

10. Anticlaudianus, carmine.—Hugonis de Pushac, Dunelmensis Episcopi, Brutus, carmine.[3]

Longiuscula forma, pergameno.

3.   This MS. is now in the Cottonian library, Vespas. A. x. "Joannes Dee, 1574, Maij 7, bowght uppon a stall in London."

11. Tractatus compendiosus de animalibus.

4° pergameno.

12. Wilhelmi Parisiensis fragment. de universis.

4° pergameno.

13. Euclidis Elementa Geometrica, Optica et Catoptrica, ex Arabico translata per Adellardum.—Theodosii Sphæricorum libri.—Liber de occultis.—Ptolomæi planisphærium.—Jordani planisphærium.—Archimedis tractatus de quadratura circuli.—Gerardi de Brussel

liber de motu.—Jordanus de ponderibus.—Libri quatuor geometriæ practicæ.—Alfarabius de scientiis.—Wilhelmi de Conchis philosophia.—Rasis liber de phisiognomia.—Anatomia hominis.—De proprietatibus elementorum.—cum aliis.

4° pergameno.

14. Augustinus de anima et spiritu.—Theoremata de spiritu et anima demonstrata.—Algorithmus demonstratus Joh. de Sacrobosco.—Joh. de Rupella summa de anima.—Rob. Lincolniensis tractatus de sphæra.—Joh. de Sacrobosco tractatus de sphæra.—Tractatus de proportione et proportionalitate, &c. Rogeri Bachonis—cum aliis.

pergameno, 4°.

15. Maximi Monachi, Dionisii Areopagitæ, Sophronii Solitarii, et aliorum Græcorum fragmenta nonnulla.

pergameno, 4°.

16. Ramundi Lullii liber de quinta essentia.

papyro, f°.

Non est Ramundi Lullii, sed collectanea diversa ex Paracelso.

17. Rogerii Bachonis de anima, et ejus operibus.—Ejusdem liber de intellectu et intelligibili.

f° pergameno.

18. Apologia de versutiis atque perversitatibus pseudo-theologorum et religiosorum.—Joachim Abbatis prophetia contra religiones tenentes ordinem mendicantium.—Arnoldi de Villa Nova opus de generibus abusionum veritatis, et de pseudo-ministris Antichristi cognoscendis, et de pastorali officio circa gregem exercendo.—Ejusdem prophetia catholica, tradens artem annihilandi versutias

Antichristi et omnium membrorum ejus, ad sacrum collegium Romanorum.

pergameno, f°.

19. Rogeri Bachonis de retardatione senectutis et senii, &c.—Ejusdem de graduatione medicinarum compositarum, &c.

pergameno, f°.

20. Ejusdem Bachonis metaphisica.—Ejusdem oeconomica.

pergameno, 4°.

21. Ejusdem[4] de animalibus fragmentum.

pergameno, f°.

4. Dee has added in the margin the word "dubito," meaning, I suppose, that there was not any sufficient evidence for attributing this treatise to Roger Bacon.

22. Ejusdem Bachonis fragmenta quædam; videlicet, de multiplicatione et corruptione specierum.—Item communia naturalia.—Epistola ad Clementem per R. de utilitate scientiarum artis experimentalis, &c.

pergameno, f°.

23. Rogeri Bachonis pars sexta Operis Majoris, quæ est Scientia Experimentalis, ad Clementem Pontif: Romanorum.—Ejusdem Operis Majoris pars septima, quæ est, Philosophia Moralis.—Ejusdem Alchimiæ tractatus expositorius, ad Clementem P.M.R.—Ejusdem compendium alchimiæ.—Avicennæ clavis sapientiæ, seu porta minor, seu tractatus de anima.—Breviloquium Holcot.—Rogerii Bachonis speculum alchimiæ.—Quæstiones super librum Jordani de ponderibus.—Compendium artis, Raymundi Lullii.—

Excerpta ex theorica Ramundi Lullii.—Rogeri Bachonis tractatus de speciebus.

papyro, f°.

24. Alberti Magni de mineralibus libri quinque.—Hermetis quadripartitum operis.—Rhithmomachia.—De lapide bezaar.—Ars fusoria ac tinctoria lapidum ac gemmarum.—Ptolomei liber de lapidibus et sigillis eorundem.—Techel de sculpturis lapidum.—Galenus (... portis) de spermate.—Avicennæ phisiognomia.—Commentariolus in Aristotelis phisiognomiam.—Cheiromantiæ fragmentum.—Arithmeticæ fragmentum, carmine.—Practica algorismi.—Anima artis transmutatoriæ Ramundi.—Phisica, seu medicina Ramundi Lullij.—De herbis.—De potentiis duodecim signorum et septem planetarum.—Epistola accurtationis lapidis philosophorum ad Regem Robertum.—Summa cheiromantiæ.—Albertus Magnus de mineralibus.—Phisiognomia ex Loxio, Aristotele, et Palemone.—Albertus de plantationibus arborum et de conservatione vini.—Virtutes septem herbarum Aristotelis.—Liber Kirimandarum.—Philonis fragmentum de aquæductibus.—Quæstiones quædam naturales.—Constantinus Medicus de coitu.—Practica puerorum.—De natura puerorum.—Introductiones astronomicæ.—Hyppocrates de pharmacis.—Hyppocrates de secretis.—Hippocratis lex.—Hippocrates de humana natura.—Hippocrates de aere, aqua, et regionibus.

pergameno, 4°.

25. Eulogium temporis, a condito orbe in annum Christi 1367, monachi cujusdem Niniani.[5]

pergameno, f°.

---

5. Now MS. Cotton. Galba, E. VIII., partially burnt by the fire. Another copy of this work is in the library of Trinity College, Cambridge, R. vii. 2.

26. Rogerii Bachonis summa, seu opus tertium, ad Clementem P.M.—Ejusdem Bachonis majoris operis pars quarta, in qua ostenditur potestas mathematicæ in scientiis atque rebus mundi hujus.—Ejusdem compendium studii theologici.—Liber præceptorum secundum Albertum.—Liber de sigillis solis in signis, secundum Hermetem.—Albertus de sigillo et annulo leonis, et ejus virtutibus.—Arnoldus de Villa Nova de sigillis duodecim signorum.

papyro, f°.

27. Rogerii Bachonis communium naturalium libri duo, quatuor sectionibus distincti.

pergameno, f°.

In boards, with clasps.

28. Alpetraugii de verificatione motuum coelestium liber.—Thebith de his quæ indigent expositione, antequam legatur Almagestum Ptolomæi.—Liber florum Albumasar.—Liber experimentorum Albumasar.—Liber practicorum geometriæ.—Jacobi Alkindi liber de aspectibus.—Petri de Dacia commentum super tractatum algorismi.—Joh. de Sacrobosco super tractatum de sphæra.—Ejusdem computus ecclesiasticus.—Wilhelmus de Aragonia in Ptolomæi centiloquium.—Ars algorismi de fractionibus.—Scripta utilia super computum manualem.—Joh: de Sicilia in canones Arzachelis de tabulis Toletanis.—Quæstiones mathematicales.[6]

pergameno, f°.

6. Now MS. Harl. 1, "Johannes Dee, 1557." A portion of this volume formerly belonged to John of London.

29. Richardi Walyngforde Abbatis S. Albani de sinubus demonstrandis, libri iv.[7]

pergameno, f°.

7. The only copies of this work now known are in the Bodleian Library, but I have not succeeded in tracing this one.

30. Johannis Massoni Monachi epistolæ.—Epistolæ de somnio Pharaonis, seu Pharaonis et Josephi epistolæ.—Alani enchiridion de planctu seu conquestu naturæ, prosa et versu.—Bernardi Silvestris Cosmographia. 8

pergameno, 4°.

8. Otho, B. IV. vid. Tann. Bibl. p. 518.   This MS. was destroyed in the fire of 1731.

31. Bartholomei Anglici breviarium, seu de proprietatibus rerum.

pergameno, f°.

32. Jordani Nemorarii +Philotechnê+, sive de triangulis, liber primus, sexaginta quatuor propositiones continens.

pergameno, 4°.

33. Rabbi Mosis liber de venenis.—Summa brevis Galeni de cura ethicæ senectutis.—Alberti de Colonia tractatus de incisionibus arborum et plantationibus earum.—Unguentum ad omnem scabiem tollendam, quod dicitur *Veni mecum*, &c.—Tractatus de ornatu faciei.—Hermetis liber de septem planetis, &c.—Rogerii Bachonis nonnulla secreta.—De factura Saxonis Gallici.—Liber de tincturis pannorum.—Liber de coloribus illuminatorum vel pictorum.—De diversis operationibus ignium.—De diversis tincturis.—Hermetis secreta.—Item, multa alia notabilia.—Item, turba philosophorum.

pergameno, 4°.

34. Experimentorum diversorum liber.—De vernisio quo utuntur scriptores.—Secreta philosophorum.—De usu virgæ visoriæ, et hujusmodi secreta multa.

papyro, 8{vo}.

35. Arnaldi de Villa Nova thesaurus secretus operationum.—Hermetis liber de lapide philosophorum.—Alfredi liber de spiritu occultato.—Rasis practica, cum aliis viginti quinque libellis variorum autorum consimilis argumenti.

papyro, 4°.

36. Ptolomæi quadripartitum, Lat.—Albumazer introductorium.—Isibradi calendarium.—Profacii Judæi almanach.—Zaëlis electiones.—De significationibus planetarum, cum aliis tractatibus.

pergameno, 4°.

37. Expositio theoricarum.—Thebith de motu octavæ sphæræ.—Jordanus de ponderibus, cum quæstionibus notabilibus super eundem.—Jacobus Alkindus de radijs, seu de causis reddendis.—An futura possunt per astra præsciri.—Nicolai Oresmi liber divinationum.—Thomæ Bravardini geometria.—Perspectiva communis Joh. de Pecham.—Dominici de Hassia quæstiones super perspectivam communem.—Euclides de speculis.—Jacobus Alkindus de umbris et causis diversitatum aspectuum.—Dominici de Clavaso practica geometriæ.—Demonstratio æqualitatis lineæ ad peripheriam circuli.—Quadratura circuli.—Expositio tractatus de sphæra, cum quæstionibus.—Algorismus in integris Joh. de Sacro-Bosco.—Algorithmus in minutiis Joh. de Lineriis.—Thomæ Bravardini tractatus proportionum.

38. Joh. de Pecham canticum pauperum.—Joh. Walensis communiloquium.—Ejusdem Walensis dietarium, locarium,

itinerarium.—Ejusdem breviloquium.—Tractatus, cujus initium est, *Supra tribus sceleribus.*—Aristotelis liber de secretis secretorum.

pergameno, 4°.

39. Liber Physiologi de natura animalium et bestiarum.

pergameno, 8°.

40. Gualteri Burlæi tractatus de potentiis animæ.

pergameno, 4°.

41. Rogerii Bachonis perspectiva.—Ejusdem de multiplicatione specierum.

pergameno, 4°.

In paste-bords, with strings.

42. Tractatuli tres de lapide philosophorum, quorum primi initium est, "Dicit philosophus," &c.
43. Vectii Valentis anthologia.—Aristoxeni musica.—Alippii musica.—Cleomedes de mundo.—Expositio astrolabii.—Hipparchus in Aratum et Eudoxum.—*Græcè omnes.*

papyro, f°.

44. Libellus antiquissimus de speculis comburentibus, cujus initium est, "De sublimiori," &c.[9]

pergameno, 4°.

[9] Now in MS. Vespas. A. II. art. 12, "Joannes Dee, 1555." This is an extremely curious and valuable tract in the history of optical science, and is similar to the curious treatise by Gogava *De speculo ustorio.* The focus of the parabola is here for the first time indicated, a circumstance which has escaped the notice of scientific historians.

45. Jordanus de ponderibus cum scholiis, cujus initium est "Omnis ponderosi."

pergameno, f°.

46. Raymundi Lullii liber de quinta essentia.

pergameno, f°.

47. Boetius de consolatione philosophiæ, in *Græcam* linguam conversus a Maximo Planude.—Catonis distica, cum scholiis Planudis, &c. *Græcè.*—Aphthonij progymnasmata, *Græcè*.

papyro, f°.

I gave this Booke to Cracovia Library, A{o}. 1584, July 28.

48. Porphirii philosophi Isagoge in Aristotelis logicam, *Græcè*.

papyro, f°.

49. Naupegia Itali cujusdam, cum figuris.

papyro, 4°.

50. Dionysii Zecharii opusculum de lapide philosophorum, *Gallicè*.

papyro, 4°.

51. Roberti Gloucestrensis chronica, *rythmo Anglico*.[10]

papyro, f°.

10. The only MS. of Robert of Gloucester's poem, answerable to this description, is in the University Library, Cambridge.

52. Hystoria Britannicorum principum a Cadowaladro Rege ad Leolinum, per Humfredum Lluyd collecta, *Anglicè*.[11]

papyro, f°.

85

11. This MS. is now in the library of the Ashmolean Museum, No. 846.

53. Variæ compositiones aquarum mercurialium et alia experimenta chemica, *Anglicè*, cujus initium est, "He that will make," &c.

papyro, 4º.

54. Varia experimenta chimica, *Anglicè*, quorum initium est, "For to make white lead."

pergameno, fº.

55. Alberti Magni summa naturalium, cujus initium est, "Philosophia dividitur."

papyro, 4º.

56. Rogerii Bachonis annotationes super Aristotelis tractatum de secretis secretorum.

pergameno, fº.

57. Phillipi Ulstadii coelum philosophorum.

impressum, fº.

58. Inventa quædam geometrica.

papyro, fº.

My owne hand, of Richard Chancellor and Thomas Topely.
59. Dumbyltoni summa.

pergameno, fº.

60. Beda de gestis Anglorum.

pergameno, 4º.

61. Euclidis geometrica.—Rogerii Bachonis perspectiva.—Aristotilis problemata.—Campani theoricæ planetarum.

               pergameno, 4°.

62. Volumina duo magna, *Hebraicè*, de astrologicis judiciis.—Alchimia Salomonis.

              papyro, f°. 2 vol.

63. Roberti Groshed, Lincolniensis episcopi, dicta; quorum initium est, "Spiritus Sanctus per os Salomonis," &c.—Ejusdem tractatus de cessatione legalium.—Ejusdem tractatus de oculo morali, una cum aliis variis.

                pergameno, f°.

64. Isaac Judæi logica, cum aliis variis consimilis argumenti, *Hebraicè*.

                 papyro, 4°.

65. Alhazen perspectiva, &c.

                pergameno, 4°.

  John Davis' spoyle.

66. Ramundi Lullii testamentum.—Ejusdem cantilena.—Ejusdem codicillus, sive vade mecum.—Ejusdem anima transmutatoria.—Annotationes super testamentum Ramundi.—Lapidarius Raymundi.—Quæstiones de Paulina Ramundi.—Quæstiones de Olympiade Ramundi.—Declaratio tabularum figuræ 5. Ramundi.—Repertorium Raymundi.—Tractatus de consideratione lapidis.—Philosophia cujusdam Ramundistæ.—Joh. Dastini chimici somnium, seu visiones, *Anglicè*.—Ramundi Lullii distinctio tertia.—Anima artis, juxta exemplar in Anglia repertum.—Apocalypsis spiritus secreti.—Ars conversionis Mercurii et Saturni in aurum et argentum, seu de aquis Theuthidis.—Aristotelis lumen luminum.—Raimundi Lullii quæstionarius arboris philosophalis.—Quæstionarius figuræ quadrangularis.—Quæstionarius figuræ

5.—Tertia distinctio juxta aliud exemplar.—Aphorismi.—Accurtatio.—Practica secreti occulti.—Opus magnum, sive opus regale.—Considerationes operis minoris.—Cantilena *Catalonicè*, cum commento.—Ars brevis, &c.

papyro, f°.

67. Ramundi Lulli speculum alchimiæ.—Ejusdem liber de quinta essentia.—Ejusdem lapidarius, scilicet de gemmis.—Joh. Dastini liber de compositione lapidis.—Ejusdem donum Dei.—Liber radicum.—Liber administrationum.—Ejusdem Dastini speculum philosophorum.—Rasis de duodecim aquis, &c.

papyro, f°.

68. Aneti filii Abraham practica medica.—Scarsati practica medicinalis, una cum aliis.

pergameno, 4°.

69. Eathelredi Abbatis Rievallis de vita Edowardi regis Anglorum et Confessoris.[12]

pergameno, 4°.

12. Now MS. Harl. 200, "Joannes Dee, 1575."

70. Roberti episcopi Lincolniensis tractatus in lingua Romana, hoc est, *veteri rithmo Gallico*, de principio creationis mundi, de medio et fine, &c.

pergameno, 4°.

71. Wilhelmi de Northfeilde expositio super librum de differentia spiritus et animæ.—Ejusdem expositio super diversa opuscula Aristolelis phisicorum.[13]

pergameno, f°.

13. Now C.C.C. Oxon. No. 235.

72. Magistri Franconis regulæ musicales, cum additionibus aliorum musicorum, collectæ a Roberto de Handlo.—Rogerii Bachonis, perspectiva, una cum aliis geometricis et astrologicis.

                 pergameno, f°.

73. Gualtheri Burlei notabilia super Porphyrii prædicabilia, et Aristotelis prædicamenta, una cum aliarum notationum libellis.

                 papyro, 4°.

74. Boetii Musica.—Hermannus Contractus de compositione astrolabii, et de ejus utilitatibus.

                 pergameno, 4°.

75. Chronica de imperatoribus seu compendium historiarum in prima monarchia Babiloniorum, in annum Christi 1266.—Joh. de Bononia summa pontificum Romanorum et imperatorum in annum Christi 1313.—Alexandri Magni ortus et res gestæ.

                 pergameno, 4°.

76. Wilhelmi Wodford, ordinis Minorum, opusculum quaestionum quarundam, contra dialogum Joh. Wycklyf a Thoma Cantuariensi archiepiscopo condemnatum.—Thomas Palmere tractatus de imaginibus, cum aliis variis.

                 papyro, 4°.

77. Collectanea quædam chimica Siberti Rhodii.

                 papyro, f°.

78. Roberti Holcot quæstiones super quatuor libros Lombardi sententiarum.—Ejusdem quæstiones de astronomia.

pergameno, 4°.

79. Arnaldi de Villa Nova liber de alchimia, cujus initium est, "Scito, fili, quod in hoc libro," una cum aliis ejusdem opusculis.

papyro, 4°.

80. Ethici philosophi cosmographia, per D. Hieronymum Stredonem Lat. conversa.

pergameno, f°.

81. Rogerii Bachonis epistolæ tres, sive scripta tria ad Joh. Parisiensem, in quibus latet sapientia mundi.—Kalid rex ad Morienum.—Gebri et Avicennæ chimica.

papyro, 4°.

82. Euclidis elementorum geometricorum libri decem.—Ejusdem perspectiva, &c. Lat.

papyro, 4°.

83. Alhazeni perspectiva, libri septem, Lat.

pergameno, f°.

84. De fabrica speculi ustorii fragmentum.—Urso de effectibus qualitatum primarum.—Liber vaccæ.—Alberti dona.—Thomas Aquinas de essentiis rerum.

pergameno, 4°.

85. Ricardi Hampole liber, qui dicitur Incendium Amoris, *Anglicè*.

pergameno, f°.

86. Alhazeni perspectiva, Lat.—Item Alfraganus, &c. Lat.

                 pergameno, f°.

87. Albumazar de judiciis astrologicis.

                 pergameno, f°.

88. Jacobi Fabri Stapulensis conclusiones phisicæ, &c. ex Aristotele excerptæ.

                 papyro, f°.

89. Joh. Eschuidi summa Anglicana, seu medicinalis.

                 pergameno, f°.

90. Bartholomæus Anglicus de proprietatibus rerum.

               pergameno, f. grandiori.

91. Jordani Nemorarii arithmetica cum commento.—Algorithmus in integris Joh. de Sacrobosco.—Algorithmus in minutiis, Joh. de Lineriis.—Campani theorica planetarum.—Nicholai Oresmi tractatus de proportionibus proportionum.[14]—Jordani tractatus de commensuratione coelestium.—Gervasii algorithmus proportionum.—Demonstrationes conclusionum astrolabii.—Tractatus de torqueto et ejus usu.—Tabulæ Alfonsi regis Castellæ.—Canones tabularum Alfonsi per Joh. de Saxonia.—Joh. de Lineriis canones tabularum primi mobilis.—Jacob Alkindus de impressionibus aeris.—Rogerii Bachonis de utilitate arithmeticæ.—Campani compostus ecclesiasticus.—Jordani algorithmus demonstratus.

                 pergameno, f°.

14. Extract from this article in MS. Bernard, 3467, where there are other extracts from MSS. in Dee's possession.

92. Helinandi Monachi Cistercien. chronicorum mundi libri XXX. hoc est, pars prima.

> pergameno, f°.

93. Francisci Catanei Diacetii paraphrasis in Aristotelem de coelo, &c.

> pergameno, f°.

94. Isidori Hispalensis liber de natura rerum, cum glosulis.—Prisciani institutio.—Bedæ versus de die judicii.

> pergameno, 4°.

95. Tractatus de figuris stellarum in octava sphæra.—Gebri libri novem de astronomia.—Almagesti libri sex abbreviati.—Jordani libri de triangulis.—Plures conclusiones Almagisti abbreviati.—Archimedis liber de curvis superficiebus.—Tractatus Albeonis.—Tabula pro locis planetarum.—Tractatus Zaphei Arzachelis, &c.—Capitula libri Almagesti.—Compendium musices ex Boetio.—Euclidis elementa geometrica.—Gebri conclusiones de astronomia.—Theodosii sphærica.—Milei de figuris sphæricis et triangulis, libri tres.—Tabulæ planetarum de radicibus et motibus.—Machumeti Bagdedini liber divisionum.—Tractatus de quinque corporibus regularibus.—Tractatus de speculis comburentibus.—Tabula domificandi, pro latitudine Oxoniens.—Tabulæ plurium latitudinum, secundum Bachecumbe.—Thebith tractatus de motu.—Tractatus de proportione circumferentiæ circuli, &c.—Tabulæ quatuor solis.

> pergameno, f°.

96. Rogeri Bachonis tractatus de virtutibus et actionibus stellarum.

> papyro, 4°.

97. Vitellionis perspectiva.[15]

                pergameno, f°.

15. Now MS. Ashm. No. 424. From a MS. note it appears that, in 1564, the Fellows of Peterhouse, at Cambridge, presented this book to Dr. Dee, in exchange for various printed books which he gave to their library. Vid. MS. C.C.C. Oxon. No. 191.

98. Theodosii sphærica.—Euclidis data, Lat.—Archimides de quadratura circuli.

                pergameno, 4°.

99. Haly de judiciis astrorum.

                pergameno, f°.

100. Boetius de consolatione philosophiæ cum commento.—Scripta super plures libros geometriæ.—Jordanus de speculis.—Jordanus de ponderibus.—Archadii demonstrationes de quadratura circuli.—Tractatus Hermanni de astrolabio.—Liber de similibus arcubus.—Archimedes de figuris isoperimetris.—Archimedes de curvis superficiebus.

                pergameno, 4°.

101. Avicenna de prima philosophia, i.e. de causa causarum, vel metaphisica, Lat.

                pergameno, 4°.

102. Alhazeni perspectiva.

                pergameno, 4°.

103. Ricardi de Posis summa epistolarum (quasi ars quædam notariatus) secundum consuetudinem Romanæ curiæ.

                pergameno, f°.

104. Arzachelis tabulæ astronomicæ.

              pergameno, 4°.

105. Chronicon Angliæ, *Anglicè*, manuscriptum.

              pergameno, f°.

106. Aristotelis commentum in astrologiam (fragmentum).

              pergameno, 4°.

107. Alberti Magni minerarium.

              pergameno, 4°.

108. Haly de judiciis astrorum.—Liber novem judicum in astrologia.—Jafar de imbribus.—Messahala de nativitatibus.—Aristotelis liber de judiciis universalibus.—Hani Benhannæ liber de geometria.—Guido Bonatus de astrologio.[16]

              papyro, f°. magno.

16. Now MS. Savil. Oxon. No. 15.

109. Algorithmus integrorum cum commento.—Algorithmus fractorum cum commento.—Summa utriusque arithmeticæ Boetii.—Arithmetica compilata ex multis scientiis.—Liber de figuris numerorum.—Practica memorandi.—Tractatus de speculo combustorio secundum sectionem Mukesij.—Euclidis geometricorum libri 15. cum commento.—Jordanus de ponderibus cum commento.—Euclides de ponderibus cum commento.—Euclidis datorum liber cum commento.—Archimedes de curvis superficiebus cum commento.—Archimedes de quadratura circuli, cum commento.—Archimedes de figuris ysoperimetrorum.—Theodosii sphærica.—Rob. Lincolniensis

episcopi, de luce, calore, et iride.—Vitellionis perspectivæ libri quatuor.

pergameno, f°.

110. Rob. Lincolnⁱensis episcopi constitutiones pro sua diocesi, videl. in decalogum, &c.

pergameno, f°.

111. Perspectiva Algazet, forte Halazen. Lat.

pergameno, 4°.

112. Annales regulorum Cambricorum, a Cadowaladro, ad Leolini tempora, *lingua Brytannica sive Cambrica.*

papyro, 4°.

113. Perquisita et alia quæ pertinebant ad Winchecumbe Abbatiam.[17]

pergameno, 4°.

---

17. It does not appear from Tanner's *Notitia Monastica*, or from Sir Thomas Phillipps's Catalogue, that this MS. is now preserved.

---

114. Boetii arithmetica.

pergameno, 4°.

115. Quæstiones erudite disputatæ super librum meteororum Aristotelis.

pergameno, 4°.

116. De Indorum et Persarum annis astronomicis.—Annotationes in Martianum Capellam.

pergameno, 4°.

117. De potentiis animæ.—Auberti Remensis philosophia.—Oliveri philosophia.—Petrus Hispanus de morte et vita, et causis longitudinis et brevitatis vitæ.—Albertus de divinatione. De spiritu et inspiratione.—De signis aquarum, ventorum et tempestatum.—Ramundus Massiliensis de cursu planetarum.—Alexander Aphrodiseus ad imperatores Antoninum et Severum de fato.—Quæstiones de intellectu.—Quæstiones de anima.—Hermannus Secundus de essentiis.—Platonis Phædon, sive de anima.—Commentum super Platonis Timæum.—Platonis Menon. Lat.

pergameno, f°.

118. De administratione principum liber.

pergameno, 4°.

119. Isidori Hispalensis etymologiarum fragmentum magnum.

pergameno, f°.

120. Tabulæ astronomicæ ad annos decem, cum canonibus.—Algorithmus demonstratus cum minutiis.—Alfraganus de annis.—Alcabicii astrologia.—Tabulæ de numeris proportionalibus.—Computus cum calendario.

pergameno, 4°.

121. Polychronica.

pergameno, f°.

122. Polychronicon.

pergameno, f° minori.

123. Hystoriæ Britannicæ et Angliæ fragmentum, *Gallicè* conscriptum.

pergameno, 4°.

124. Guido Bonatus de judiciis astrorum.

                 pergameno, f°.

125. Passionale.

                 pergameno, f°.

126. Astronomici libelli cujusdam fragmentum, cujus initium est, "A philosophis astronomiam sic definitam accepimus."

                 pergameno, 4°.

127. Expositio quædam super Cantica Canticorum.—Ars fidei secundum Ambionensem.—Macrobius in somnium Scipionis.

                 pergameno, f°.

 The second tract is cut out, and to be answered for.

128. Matricula, sive catalogus bibliothecæ Cantuariensis.

                 papyro, f°.

129. Author de causis cum demonstrationibus.

                 pergameno, f°.

130. Alchimicus libellus, *Anglicè*, cujus initium est, "Take limale."

                 papyro, 4°.

131. Libellus chimicus, *Latinè*.—Varii tractatus super capitulum Hermetis quod dicitur "Clavis Sapientiæ Majoris."

                 pergameno, f°.

132. Sidrach philosophi liber, *Gallicè*.

                 pergameno, 4°.

133. Kallendarium.—Quædam de computu ecclesiastico, *Latinè et Saxonicè*.—Alphabetum somniale.—Præces quædam piæ.[18]

pergameno, 8°.

18. The MS. described by Wanley, p. 222, as MS. Cotton. Vitell. A. XVIIJ. now destroyed, is probably the one here mentioned. The Cotton. MS. Jul. A. VJ. also answers the brief description above given.

134. Lectiones cujusdam super Ecclesiasticen.

pergameno, f°.

135. Commentarius bonus in definitiones quinti libri Euclidis.—Euclides totus ex Campani traditione.—Explicatio bona Archimedis de quadratura circuli.

pergameno, 4°.

136. Cicero de natura deorum.—Catonis liber ad Varronem.—Euclidis liber cum commento.—Preceptum canonum Ptolomæi.—Tractatus astrolabii duplicis cum practica.—Tabulæ astronomicæ.—Aristotelis epistola de rectitudine vitæ, ad Alexand.—Henrici Britton philosophia.—Oliveri Britton philosophia.—Philosophia Remensis et aliorum.—Liber de speculis, liber de visu, et quædam alia.

pergameno, 4°.

137. Boetii arithmetica.—Ejusdem de trinitate libri.—Ejusdem de duobus in Christo naturis.—Ejusdem de hebdomadibus.—Rob. Grostesti, Lincolniensis episcopi, de arte algorismi communi.—Ejusdem alius tractatus magis in speciali.—Thebith super Almagistum Ptolomæi.—Theodosius de locis habitabilibus.—Theoria planetarum cum tabulis necessariis.—Commentum super Centiloquium Ptolomæi.—Ars cheiromantiæ, *in Gallico*

sermone.—De interpretationibus somniorum.—De significationibus tonitruorum.—Physiognomia secundum Thomam Aquinatem.—De prognosticationibus tempestatum.—De pluribus necessariis ad casus inquirendos secundum algorismum.—Cheiromantia, Lat.[19]

pergameno, 4°.

19. Now in Trinity College, Dublin. See Dr. Bernard's Catalogue, No. 46.

138. Astronomica, astrologica, et arithmetica.—Observationes quædam planetarum et fixarum, Petri de Sancto Audomaro et Joh. de Lineriis.

pergameno, 4°.

139. Tabulæ astronomicæ cum canonibus.

pergameno, 8°.

140. Libellus de natura locorum.

pergameno, 8°.

141. Ivonis Carnutensis varii tractatus ecclesiastici, et volumen epistolarum diversorum ad diversos, &c.

pergameno, f°.

142. Boetii musica.—Expositio Simonis de Bredon super duos libros arithmeticæ Boetii.

pergameno, 4°.

143. Calcidius in Platonis Timæum.[20]

pergameno, 4° long.

20. Now MS. Bib. Reg. Mus. Brit. 12. B. XXII, "Johannes Dee, 1557, 4. Maij, Londini."

144. Marii de elementis libri duo.—Liber qui dicitur Prenonphysicon.—lardi Bathoniensis quæstiones naturales.—Physiognomia secundum tres authores, videlicet, Loxum, Aristotelem, et Palemonem.—Liber spermatis.—Soranus de re medica.—Constantini liber de herbis.—Dioscorides de virtutibus herbarum, Lat.—Oribasius de virtutibus herbarum, Lat.—Odonis Adunensis versus de virtutibus herbarum.—Isidori Hyspalensis etymologiarum libri.—Constantini Medici liber graduum.—Euphonis experimenta.—Adamarii experimenta.—Joh. Melancholici experimenta.—Experimenta Abbatis.—Experimenta Wiscardi.—Experimenta Picoti.—De urina mulieris.—Expositio quintæ incisionis epidemiarum Hippocratis.—Joh. Melancholici liber de substantia urinæ.—Palladius de agricultura.—Liber de simplici medicina.

pergameno, fº.

145. Alberti Magni magia naturalis et vera.—Idiotæ liber, authore Cusano.—Contra Jacobellinos in Bohemia.—Antonii Barsizii cauteriaria, comedia, una cum aliis variis.

papyro, fº.

146. Aristotelis physicorum libri octo.—Ejusdem de generatione et corruptione, lib. 2.—De coelo et de mundo, libri 4.—Meteorum libri 4.—De vegetabilibus, &c.—De anima, libri tres.—De memoria et reminiscentia.—Ethicorum secundus et tertius.—De morte et vita, et alia ejusdem Aristotelis, Latinè.

pergameno, 4º.

147. Serapionis de aptatione et repressione, seu servitor Serapionis.

pergameno, fº.

148. Thomas de Aquino de veritate theologica, libri septem.

pergameno, 4º.

149. Alberti magni tractatus de lapidibus.—Jacobus Alkindus de radiis.
papyro, f°.

150. Historia Anglica cujusdam anonymi.
papyro, 4°.

151. Euclidis optica, catoptrica, et geometria, Lat.
pergameno, 4°.

152. Fragmentum theologicum quoddam in Ecclesiasticum.
pergameno, f°.

153. Tractatus astrolabij.—De significatione rei occultæ.—De aeris dispositione.—Tabula pro almanack.—Ars notaria.—Aristotelis epistola de conservatione sanitatis.—Rogeri Herefordensis computus.—Compositio astrolabii.—Planisphærium.—Alfraganus.—Geber in Ptolomæi almagestum, una cum aliis.
pergameno, 4°.

154. Apologia chemicæ artis, contra Cornelium Agrippum de vanitate scientiarum.—De oleis variis medicinalibus, una cum aliis multis.
papyro, 4°.

155. Alcabicius.—Astronomia quædam judicialis.—Zahelis introductorium, cum judiciis sequentibus.—Mathematica Alexandri summi astrologi.—Jacob Alkindus de judiciis astrologicis.—Albumazar de revolutionibus annorum mundi.—Summæ excerptæ ex libro Albumazar, de revolutione nativitatum.—Albohali de nativitatibus.—Albumazar liber florum.—Almanack perpetuum Profacii Judæi.—Thomas Aquinas de angelis.[21]
4° pergameno.

21. This MS. is now in the Ashmolean collection, No. 360.

156. Lamentationes Mathæoluli, carmine.[22]

pergameno, 4°.

22. This is probably the copy now in MS. Cotton. Cleopatra, C. IX. I know of no other which answers the description.

157. Hippocratis aphorismi.—Ejusdem prognostica.—Ejusdem liber de regimine acutorum.—Ejusdem liber epidemiarum.—Ejusdem astronomia de infirmitatibus.—Johannicii isogoge in Galeni Tecknin.—Hyppocratis secreta.—Tractatus de compositione astrolabii.—Tractatus de practica astrolabii.—Tractatus de compositione novi quadratis.—Campani tractatus de motibus planetarum et de fabricatione equatorii instrumenti per quod certa loca planetarum inveniuntur.—Petri Perigrini tractatus de magnete.[23]—Jordani liber Planisphærii.—Euclidis liber de speculis.—Jordani tractatus de ponderibus.—Practica geometriæ.

pergameno, 4°.

23. Dee's own copy of the printed edition, with his MS. notes, is in the British Museum. "Johannes Dee, 1562."

158. Rogerii Bachonis calendarium.—Tabula ad sciendum quis planeta dominetur omni hora cujus libet diei.—Tabula multiplicationis.—Liber de naturis rerum abreviatus.—Marbodeus de sculpturis gemmarum.—Liber de lapidibus filiorum Israel.—Hippocratis signa in infirmo.—Unguentum alabastri.—De modo faciendi olei.—De aquis mundificativis oculorum faciei, et aliorum spiritualium membrorum.—De pilatoria.—Ut pili nascantur ubi

volueris.—De conservatione vini.—Gregorii dialogorum liber primus et secundus.—Vita Sancti Nicholai.—Vita Sancti Ægidij.

pergameno, 4°.

159. Computus ecclesiasticus.—Beda de calculatione.—Computus.

pergameno, 4°.

160. Wilhelmi de Conchis philosophia.[24]

pergameno, 4°.

24. Now MS. Bib. S. Joh. Coll. Cantab. G. 3. "Johannes Dee, 1557, 4. Maii."

161. Quæstiones super elenchos, et alia logicalia.

papyro, 4°.

162. Quæstiones de apparentiis, seu fallaciis sophisticis, manuscriptæ.

papyro.

163. Alberti de Saxonia tractatus proportionum, 4° impressus Rothomagi.—Jacobi Lupi tractatus de productionibus personarum in divinis, secundum mentem Joh. Scoti, 4° impressum.—Una cum aliis tractatibus variarum quæstionum,—

papyro manuscript. 4°.

164. Henrici Beaumundi regimen sanitatis, cum aliis variis experimentis, tam *Anglicè* quam Latinè scriptis.

pergameno, 4°.

165. Avicenna de naturalibus.—Ejusdem de sufficientia.—Thomæ de Aquino tractatus de essentia.—Avendauth de quinque universalibus.—Alchindi philosophi de quinque essentiis, ex verbis Aristotelis abstractus liber.—Platonis Timæus.—Isaac de diffinitionibus, Lat.—Jacob de rationali in anima.—Alexandri

Philosophi de intellectu et intelligibili liber, Lat.—Algacelis logica.—Alchindus de intellectu et intellecto.—Amaometh liber introductorius in artem logicam demonstrationis.—Averrhois de substantia orbis.—Alfarabius de intellectu et intellecto.—Liber planetarum cujusdam discipuli Ptolomæi.—Mercurius Trismegistus.—Secundus Philosophus de diffinitionibus.—Boetius de unitate.—Liber de differentia spiritus et animæ.—Liber metaphisicæ Avicennæ, qui non est completus.

166. De philosophia Salomonis.—Fulgentius episcopus ad Calcidium Grammaticum.—Experimenta quædam alchimica.—Cassiodorus de anima, una cum aliis theologicis.

pergameno, 8°.

167. Boetii arithmetica.—Theorica planetarum et stellarum secundum Alfraganum.—Boetii musica.—Euclidis geometrica.—Propositiones planisphærii Ptolomæi cum additionibus.—Maslem Arabis.[25]

pergameno, 4°.

25. Now MS. Lambeth, No. 67.   Dee's autograph has been erased from the fly-leaf, but "1558, 30.   Junii, Londini," remains in his handwriting.

168. Disputatio inter militem et clericum.

pergameno, 4°.

169. Joh. Scoti quæstiones super secundo et tertio libro Aristotelis de anima.—Antonii Andreæ quæstiones in Aristotelis meteora.

papyro, 4°.

170. Isidori Hispalensis liber differentiarum.—Cic. academicæ quæstiones.—Ejusdem natura deorum.—Ejusdem de divinatione.—Ejusdem de fato.—Ejusdem paradoxa.—Ejusdem Philippicæ

orationes.—Libellus de bestiis, avibus, et arboribus.—Salustius de bello Catilinario et Jugurthino.—Vegetius de re militari, &c.

pergameno, 4°.

171. Computus Ecclesiasticus.

pergameno, 8°.

172. Solinus de mirabilibus mundi.

pergameno, 4°.

173. Bona gesta Mariæ.—Maleus, &c.

pergameno, 16°.

174. Sortilegia nugatoria.

pergameno, 8°.

175. Sortilegia nugatoria.

pergameno, 4°.

176. Joh. Sarisberiensis policraticum, sive de nugis curialium et vestigiis philosophorum, libri octo.

pergameno, 4°.

177. Computus manualis, cum aliis sexaginta quinque tractatibus variorum autorum in medicinalibus, physicis, astronomicis, et aliis.

pergameno, 8°.

178. Gebri summa alchimiæ.

pergameno, 4°.

179. Hermetis cujusdam libellus de rebus universalibus.

                 pergameno, 4°.

180. Imago mundi, cujus initium est, "Operatio divina."

                 pergameno, 4°.

181. Thomæ Bravardini Anglici propositiones geometriæ.

                 pergameno, 4°.

182. Macer de virtutibus herbarum.

                 pergameno, 4°.

183. Libellus medicinæ et chirurgiæ, partim Latinè, partim *Anglicè*, partim etiam *Gallicè*.

                 pergameno, 16°.

184. Ramundi Lulii practica chimica, *Anglicè*.[26]

                 papyro, 4°.

26. Now MS. Sloan. 2128.

185. Alchimica; videlicet tres tractatus alchimici, Volvi lapidem, &c.—De quinta essentia Mercurii.—Secretum secretorum Pleri philosophi.

                 pergameno, 4°.

186. Roberti Lincolniensis episcopi, de luce, de iride, cum multis aliorum tractatis circiter 34.

                 pergameno, 4°.

  A thick booke with a labell.

187. Libri diversi astrologici, quoram primi initium est, "Postulata a Domino."

pergameno, 4°.

188. Rogeri Bachonis, Morieni Romani, Joh. Viennensis, Alberti Magni, Hermetis, Rasis, Hortulani, chimica quædam.

pergameno, 8°.

189. Speculum secretorum, cum aliis haud contemnendis chemicis fragmentis.

pergameno, 4°.

190. Joh. de Sacrobosco sphæra.—Johannicii glossulæ, cum aliis tractatibus.—Rogeri Bachonis et Rob. Lincolniensis episcopi, &c.

pergameno, 4°.

191. Libellus chimicus, cujus initium est, "Materia lapidis."

papyro, 8°.

192. Jacobi Alkindi de pluviis, imbribus, ventis, et de mutatione aeris.

papyro, f°.

193. Liber duodecim aquarum, &c.[27]

pergameno, 4°.

27. Now in Magdalen College, Oxford, No. 277.

194. Ægidii de Wallecers computus, de cometis, de crepusculis.—Tabulæ domorum et ascensionum.—Kallendarii errores.—Jo. de

Pecham perspectiva communis.—30. Arabes, qui dicuntur Magistri probationum.—Tractatus minutiarum, una cum aliis.

pergameno, 8°.

195. Abraham Judæi liber de judiciis nativitatum, cum aliis variis.

papyro, 4°.

196. Albertus de mineralibus, cujus initium est, "De mixtione et coagulatione," &c.—Rogerii Bachonis epistola prima ad Joh. Parisiensem.—Summa aurea, una cum multorum aliorum tractatibus.

pergameno, 4°.

In a black cover with clasps.
197. Ludus astronomicus.

papyro, 8°.

198. Parisiensis liber, cujus initium est, "Augustinus de Civitate Dei," &c.

papyro, 4°.

199. Pomum Ambræ.—Trotulæ de ornatu mulierum.—Ascarus Philosophus de signis mulierum.—De secretis mulierum, cum aliis experimentis.—Theophilus Monachus de coloribus.—Eraclius de coloribus et artibus Roman.—Quædam experimenta medica, cum aliis superstitiosis.—Compositio et usus astrolabii, una cum aliis.

pergameno, 8°.

[*In that part of the Catalogue describing the printed Books, under the title of "Chemici Libri, &c. Compacti," occur the following Manuscripts.*]

200. Ramundi Lulii ars generalis, cum quæstionibus ejusdem.—De medicina et astronomia ejusdem.—Speculum medicinæ.

4°.

201. Ramundi Lulii ars magna cum figuris.—Ejusdem ars generalis, cum quæstionibus.—Ejusdem introductorium sive canones artis generalis.—Ejusdem de principiis et medicinæ gradibus.—Ejusdem de regiminibus sanitatis et infirmitatis.

f°.

A CATALOGUE OF SUCH OF DR. DEE'S MSS. AS ARE COME TO MY HANDS.

[By Elias Ashmole.][28]

28. From Ashmole's MSS. No. 1790, fol. 52ª.]

1. Mysteriorum liber primus, 1581, et 1582.
    It begins 22. Dec. 1581, and ends 15. March 1582.
2. Mysteriorum liber secundus.
    The first leafe is utterly perished. It ends 21. March, 1582.
3. Mysteriorum liber tertius.
    It begins 28. April 1582, and ends 4. May, following.
4. Liber Mysteriorum quartus.
    It began 15. Nov. 1582, but the first leafe is lost. It ends 21. Nov. following.
5. Liber Mysteriorum quintus, 1583.
    It begins 23. March 1583, and ends 18. April following.
6. Quinti libri Mysteriorum appendix.
    It begins 20. April 1583, and ends 23. May following.
    Note that some other of his bookes were set forth by Dr. Casaubon 1659, and the first action (in them) begins 5 daies after the last action of the foresaid appendix, viz. 28. May 1583, Which are these that follow.
7. Liber sexti Mysteriorum (et sancti) parallelus novalisque.
    It begins 28. May 1583, and ends 4. July following.

8. Liber Peregrinationis Primæ (sexti Mystici paradromus).
It begins 21. Sept. 1583, and ends 13. March 1584.
9. Mensis Mysticus Sabbaticus, pars prima ejusdem. It begins 10. April 1584, and ends the 30 of that moneth.
10. Libri Mystici Apertorii Cracoviensis Sabbatici 1584.
But in Dr. Dee's MS. (from which it was printed) it hath this title,
Libri septimi Apertorii Cracoviensis, Mystici Sabbatici, pars tertia, A{o}. 1584.
And beside hath this note, Liber quartus decimus.
The first action in this booke begins 7. May 1584, and ends 22. May following.
11. Libri Septimi Apertorij Cracoviensis Mystici Sabbatici pars quarta.
It begins 23. May 1584, and ends 12. July following.
12. Libri Cracoviensis Mysticus Apertorius.
In the originall MS. it hath this marginall note, "Sive potius, pars quinta libri 7{mi} &c. Cracoviensis."
The first action in this booke begins 12. July 1544, and ends 15. August following.
13. Mysteriorum Pragensium liber primus Cæsareusque.
It begins 15. Aug. stilo novo, 1584. At the bottome of the first leafe in the MS. is written, Liber 19us.
The last action in this booke is the 7th of Oct. 1584.
14. Mysteriorum Pragensium Confirmatio.
The first action begins 14. Jan, 1585, and ends the 20 of March following.
15. Mysteriorum Pragensium Confirmatorum liber.
This booke begins 20. Mar. 1585, and ends 6. June following.
16. Unica Actio; quæ Pacciæna vocatur. A{o}. 1585, Aug. 6.
17. Liber Resurectionis, to which the MS. adds, et 42. Mensium Fundamentum.
It begins the 30 of April 1586.

Actio prima et secunda ex septem: is also added in MS. The last action in this booke is 21. Jan. 1587.

18. Actio tertia. Mysteriorum divinorum memorabilia, ab actionis (ex septem) tertiæ, descriptæ exordio, cui dies 4° Aprilis, A{o} 1587, dicata fuit.

It begins 4. April 1587, and ends 23. May following.

Thus far from the Printed Booke.

OTHER MANUSCRIPTS.

19. 48. Claves Angelicæ.

    This booke is writen in the Angelick language. Interlined with an English translation.

    Cracoviæ ab Aprilis 13 ad Julii 13 (diversis temporibus) receptæ, A{o}. 1584. At the bottom of the title page. Liber 18.
20. Liber Scientiæ, Auxilii et Victoriæ Terrestris.

    Maij 2, stilo novo, 1585 collectus ex præmissis in lib. 10, et aliis.
21. De Heptarchia Mystica Collectaneorum, Lib: primus.
22. Liber Enoch. I suppose Liber Logaeth and this are all one, but in the MS. I copied myne from (which I borrowed from Sir John Cotton) it hath this Title, Liber Mysteriorum Sextus et Sanctus, Liber 8.
23. A Booke of Supplications and Invocations.

BIBLIOBAZAAR

The essential book market!

Did you know that you can get any of our titles in large print?

Did you know that we have an ever-growing collection of books in many languages?

**Order online:
www.bibliobazaar.com**

Find all of your favorite classic books!

Stay up to date with the latest government reports!

At BiblioBazaar, we aim to make knowledge more accessible by making thousands of titles available to you- *quickly and affordably*.

Contact us:
BiblioBazaar
PO Box 21206
Charleston, SC 29413

LaVergne, TN USA
01 March 2010

174581LV00007B/96/P